| AUTHOR | CLASS |
|--------|-------|
| CAMPBELL, K. | F A |

| TITLE | No. |
|-------|-----|
| Death descending | 17610775 |

a30118  022821908b

# DEATH DESCENDING

Fallowlands – an isolated house basking in midsummer heat, the air heavy with flower scents, and a naked girl sunbathing on a balcony roof.

A Garden of Eden? Or a jungle?

Living at Fallowlands, watching from time to time the aircraft coming in to land at Grantwick Airport, is a typical English family with all the tensions and misunderstandings of one generation against another: Professor Greville, peace-loving and tolerant; Richard, his adolescent son, war lover and weapons expert; his wife Mary, pillar of the Women's Institute; and three attractive daughters, one just left school, one an art student, one married to a pilot and expecting their first child.

And camping in the woods, an unseen stranger who also watches the planes landing at Grantwick and will some day come knocking at the door . . .

The way entry is gained to Fallowlands, the purpose for which the family is held captive, the way they work out what is happening, is beautifully described. But what is outstanding about *Death Descending* is the interplay of vivid characters, the action proceeding naturally and inevitably, as in Karen Campbell's other novels, to a tremendous and terrifying climax.

Behind this tensely exciting story is a question that may some day face all of us: how do we act if we find ourselves in the jungle of the world today?

*by the same author*

WHEEL FORTUNE

THUNDER ON SUNDAY

SUDDENLY, IN THE AIR

# death descending

## Karen Campbell

COLLINS St James's Place, London, 1976

For David

William Collins Sons & Co Ltd
London · Glasgow · Sydney · Auckland
Toronto · Johannesburg

First published 1976
© Karen Campbell, 1976

ISBN 0 00 222444 5
Set in Linotype Pilgrim

Made and Printed in Great Britain by
William Collins Sons & Co Ltd Glasgow

# approach

Rowena Greville opened the back door, unlocked as usual, and flung her ridiculous prefect's hat on to the scrubbed kitchen table. The house had an empty feel. Its ancient quiet dropped around her as palpable and shielding as a dark silk robe. The only sound, for the moment, was the tick of the antique wooden clock above the Aga. Not the squeak of a board nor the scurry of a mouse.

Alone! Hallelujah and *bellissima,* she thought, reaching a glass from the dresser, opening the fridge and pouring herself some home-made lemonade. All the way along the lane and then down the long hot sandy track to the house, she had thought of its bitter coldness. She rolled it round her mouth, the way her father did when he wished to appear knowledgeable about brandy. *Quelle charade!*

It was almost midsummer. The sun shone with an un-

English brightness and constancy. Typical A-level weather! In a week's time, *après* the exams *le déluge*. Rowena frowned at the sunlit garden, blazing with vibrant colour, colour behind the latticed sound-proofed windows, courtesy of the Airport's Authority. Then she washed up her glass (her mother only had help once a week and the house was large) and climbed the staircase to her room.

It was on the west side of Fallowlands, all beams and white paint like the rest of it. And because (when her parents had bought the place very cheap because of its isolated and undesirable situation) a flat-roofed utility room had been added, Rowena's room boasted a balcony with french doors leading on. The most secret and undisturbed place in this most secret and undisturbed house. Thick walls, overhanging gables, Tudor tiling, small inscrutable windows gave the house, when one eventually found it amongst its screening cupressus and elms and giant rhododendrons, an oddly furtive look. Yet its cheapness had nothing to do with its furtive look, but to a fact undreamed of by the Tudor master builder who erected it, whose initials were still carved on some of the roof timbers, the bull-nosed bricks and the kitchen floor flagstones. Fallowlands now stood on the approach path to the newly extended main runway at Grantwick, at a point where the incoming aircraft with unfailing accuracy lowered flaps and boosted their power.

But all in all, a tolerable drawback for such a house. For there was nothing furtive inside. Gay curtains, bowls of flowers, home-grown plants, carefully covered cushions. Her mother, once the Redbrick hope (Professor Greville's favourite student, no less and certainly no more), her mother was now the graduate of the Women's Institute par excellence.

A bottler, an embroiderer, a flower-arranger, a maker of omelettes out of garden horrors that more fortunate ladies threw away. She had given up all her love and motherhood in the fashion of her benighted day. And now lived unhappily ever after.

*Quelle douleur!* Rowena murmured aloud, and stopped to sniff a clever arrangement of nicotiana and rue.

Her bedroom door was slightly ajar. She pushed it open further, unzipping her cotton school dress as she walked across the big cool room. Half way to the bed, she stopped in her tracks. Out of the corner of her eye, she had caught a movement from the balcony.

She was not alone. She swore under her breath, crept stealthily over and wrenched open the french doors.

Ginny, her twenty-two-year-old sister, didn't stir. She was lying naked on an orange bath towel, still as a statue, though infinitely and unfairly more beautiful. Ginny's small pointed face was turned up hungrily to the sun, her eyes invisible behind fashionable large gold-framed sunglasses.

'Christ! *Gott in Himmel!*' Rowena exclaimed in genuine outrage. 'How can you just lie like that?'

The pointed face remained fixed. The full lips moved just enough to murmur.

'Very comfortable, thank you, child. But you could throw me one of your pillows if you really insist.'

'Bloody hell! I'd put it over your mouth if I did.'

'That I quite believe.'

'*Sacré bleu!* What in God's name are you doing on my bloody balcony?'

The lips moved to a condescending smile. 'Why, moongazing, child!'

Rowena prodded her sister's thigh with the toe of her massive school shoe. 'Don't try to be clever!'

'It comes naturally, sweetie.'

'That is the laugh of the century.'

'Then laugh. It would make a change.'

'I'm not in the mood.'

'You're never in the mood.' Ginny suddenly sat up and whipped off her sunglasses, disclosing eyes of a curious, devastatingly attractive shade of sea green. She stared at her sister with passing concern. Ginny was the beauty of the family. Eleanor, the eldest, had (according to her father and quite inaccurately according to Rowena) both beauty and brains. Richard miracle child coming after three daughters and a miscarriage, the answer to a prayer had the family not been too liberal and enlightened to believe in such mumbo-jumbo, was the Enigma. Now aged sixteen, he was perhaps the only subject on which the three sisters spoke as with one voice.

'How was the exam?'

'Expectedly bloody.'

'Finish it?'

'Just.'

'You'll be all right then.' Ginny yawned, losing interest, and stretch her nut-brown body like a cat. Rowena watched her with mingled envy and disgust.

'And take your filthy shoe off my perfect skin. Otherwise I'll have spots.'

'Where's Mum?'

'Darby and Joan outing. Wheeling ancients down to Ramsgate.'

'Richard?'

'Rifle Club.'

'Did Our Father weaken then?'

'So it would seem.'

'A truly tolerant man must even tolerate intolerance,' Rowena mimicked, and had the satisfaction of seeing Ginny give an involuntary smile.

'By the way,' she said, leaning closer, 'you've got a whole lot of nasty little spots on your chest.'

'Liar!' Ginny peered down at her small, perfectly shaped breasts, explored the skin of her chest carefully and then brought her hand down with a smart crack on her sister's leg. 'And take your filthy great boot off my peach skin.'

Rowena prodded deeper. 'For that matter, take your filthy

indecent body off my balcony!'

'Why should I?'

'Because I say so.' She swung her foot back and gave her sister's thigh a sharp kick. 'Someone might see you.'

With her hand raised Ginny suddenly burst out laughing. 'Here! Some sex-starved squirrel? Or randy rabbit? I tell you we could all die in the night and no one would ever know.' She clasped her arms round her knees and stared out moodily at the dark summer-green tops of the trees. Absorbed, as Ginny was apt to become at times, in some inner shadow of her own.

Then her eye was caught by the silver shape of a descending aircraft, harmless and silent as a minnow in the clear blue sky before its sound wave travelled to them. They watched it swell in the seemingly unresistant air.

'That's the twenty-fifth I've counted!' Ginny exclaimed, clapping her hands over her ears as the crescendo of noise enveloped them like a tide. Faintly the latticed windows shook and tinkled. Ginny's tin of sun oil danced towards the edge of the flat roof.

'Which shows how bloody long you've lazed up here!' Rowena shouted, kicking the tin of sun oil over the edge with sudden whole-hearted rage. 'You could at least have got some tea ready!'

She felt overwhelmed with an inexplicable anger that had nothing really to do with the sweet lazy good-humoured Ginny. Something to do with the shadow of that landing aircraft as it went, covering Ginny's body in a dark cross like the headstone of a grave.


Other families must be hell too. Rowena kicked at the little mole mounds on the sunbaked lawn. The garden was heavy with the scent of summer flowers. Hot even in the shadow of the shrubs. Crickets rasped in the coarser grass nearer the paddock. Bees droned, heavily languid with nectar. A land flowing with milk and honey. On the surface. While below? What was below? The pruning knife and the sting?

She sighed. No, it wasn't fair. In their own little encapsulated way they were a happy enough family surely? Not the Oxo gravy Browning family mark. But happy. And modestly successful. Father a history professor at a minor college of London University. More firsts and upper seconds to his credit than most. An inspiring teacher, some said. Mother an exemplary if slightly deflating wife, devoted to her three daughters and her son, well respected, loyal friend, though few close friends to be loyal to. I am airing their obituaries, she thought in sudden guiltiness and alarm. She clicked the gate between the empty paddock and the garden shut tight behind her. But her thoughts on the family refused to be snapped off.

The trouble was, they lacked leadership. She despised, though her schoolfriends envied, her father's so-called liberal outlook. It irritated her like loose knicker elastic. Made her nervous. And nervousness came out in her as aggression. She was only too aware of the vast tempestuous sea of the headmistress's favourite hymn. She would have liked a few charts for life. Or even the odd windmill to fling her cap over.

Within the family there were few rules and, though her mother went intermittently to church, no rigidly held beliefs. Other than in the basic decency of the human race. A belief which six years travelling on the school bus had made Rowena discount. Eleanor, Ginny and Rowena had always been allowed to come in at what time they wanted, and have what boy-friends they could muster. None so far in Rowena's case. She was plain. She was a late emotional developer. And she had a slight problem with what her father called puppy fat. Sex was of course discussed freely.

'Have you taken a lover yet?' Father had asked Eleanor three months after starting her job as a harassed receptionist at Grantwick Airport. A question which had no doubt hastened her into a middle-class solitaire-gemmed engagement announced in the *Telegraph,* followed at a decorous interval by a white C. of E. wedding to her jolly red-faced pilot. A strapping extrovert, as unlike her father as any man could hope to be.

In much the same way Father's obsessive pacifism had given Richard his passion for guns and all things military. *Eheu. Eheu,* Rowena sighed. And now Richard had been allowed to join the Rifle Club, and next week Eleanor was going to come home for a bit of looking after while husband was away. Disgustingly in pod, and inviting horribly frank conversations, which frankly had put Rowena off sex for the rest of her natural life. Yet she was aware of passions and emotions inside herself which cried for some outlet. Almost a bearing down pain of her emergent womanhood.

Rowena paused in her ambling walk down the paddock towards the strip of wood. She looked up as another aircraft came over, stood with her arms wide as it swept its cruciform shadow over the rough unusable grass. When she'd been younger, and there weren't so many aircraft coming in to Grantwick, she used to wave.

Imagining romantically that a helmeted and begoggled figure might see her. Fall in love. Take her away. Now she knew that pilots were red-faced and beefy, ate too much, worried about themselves, their health and their wives having babies, joined the Round Table, and that all they ever saw were the runway lights and their instruments. She watched it skim the wood. The thick toxic exhaust hung in a black feather over the tree-tops, swirled behind the aircraft as it banked like an angel fish's tail. Then the diminished silver shape dropped out of sight. Seconds later she heard the great roar of its reverse thrust (beefy Brother-in-Law had explained) as it landed. And with thankfulness for momentary silence, she jumped the fence that held back the wood.

It was like a deep green pool standing above ground, its darkness and chill as startling as sliding into cold stagnant water. It had its depths of dark and its shallows of lambent light.

She could feel the shock of its chill on her bare arms. She drew in the deep sappy smell of vegetation mixing with the smell of the narrow half-dried-up stream at the bottom. She blinked her eyes at the needles of bright sun lancing down through the thick tough roof of leaves.

Because of the exams, it was weeks since she had been down here. The leaves had lost their innocent spring green. The chlorophyll had darkened in them like old blood.

Perhaps, looking back on it, she knew even then that like her room her privacy had been violated.

She waited for a moment, listening. Somewhere high in one of the beeches, a blackbird chirped its urgent repetitive warning. A mouse or a thrush scuffed and sorted in last autumn's rotted leaves. Birds sang, robins or thrushes, she could never tell which, though she liked to pretend that she could. Wood pigeons cooed their Greek chorus of muted apprehension.

She shrugged at her own ridiculous sensitivities, and began kicking the brambles aside, noisily thrusting her way deeper in. Immediately the pigeons rose in clapping flight. Whatever was to begin was to begin.

This wood, like the paddock, was all part of Fallowlands' enclosing acres, though rarely did anyone, except occasionally Richard, come here other than herself. Occasionally she picked the blackberries for her mother to make jam, found specimens for Botany or to draw for Art. The blackberries were in flower now, their delicate petals standing out in a pale pink incandescence against the jungly darkness of the summer wood.

It was a rough old place really. Untended, unpruned, the trees too close, overgrown, choked with ivy, weaker ones dying and resting against one another to form little hidey-holes roofed with creeper, or falling in the trickle of stream, making dammed-up rusty black pools. Her sisters had been too adult but Rowena had played down here with Richard for want of anyone better. Till the little bastard had hit a young rabbit with his air-gun.

Of all the family, he was the one she could least understand. The parents' dream-turned-nightmare. She doubted if any of them understood him. Self-willed, destructive. Vicious even. A child only a mother could love, alas and alack. She prayed that the law of genetics would be recessive and that Eleanor would not produce his double when her time came five months hence.

Standing now just above the hollow, she could see the exact place where he shot it. The rabbit had been running under that birch tree, parallel with the bed of the stream. Its fur marvellously dappled in the scatter of sunlight. It had jumped in the air, then keeled over and lain with its paws gently folded, unbelievably dead.

Rowena caught her breath. It was as if she had fallen through some crack in time. Or raised the past like the dead. I am the female adolescent acknowledgedly capable of raising poltergeists and fearful things. For the rabbit was still there. Except that the intervening years had deprived it of its head. She scrambled slowly and reluctantly down towards it. Sunlight dappled her face and dazzled her eyes as it had done the rabbit's. She felt a frightening empathy. Then closer to, she saw it wasn't a rabbit at all. Not any more, just the skin, recently gutted and neatly laid aside. Gypsies most likely. Gathering for the raspberry picking. The fur was still faintly warm. The blood not yet matted. She straightened, rubbing her hands together, conscious of a tingle of apprehension, primitive and unreasonable. Her eye caught something else, a little deeper into the hollow, a little further back from the stream and sheltered by the rise of the wood behind it, something smooth and dark. Nothing more harmful than two pieces of black polythene, each held down by a surround of small stones. She picked her way forward, and lifted the corner of the first one, disclosing a small makeshift fireplace. Rusty rods of iron laid across flat stones. Twigs and paper all ready for lighting. A clean frying pan, a battered metal casserole dish. The lid on, but she knew what was inside.

Under the other was the makings of a bed. Bracken stuffed into plastic bags to make mattress and pillow. A brown blanket of some strange-looking material carefully folded.

Someone living here. Had lived for the last few days by the look of it. Had killed and cooked and eaten and cleaned up after himself. Vanished and returned. The tremor of fear sharpened quite illogically into one of momentary terror. It was all suddenly childish and terrible. A Grimm's fairy tale. Grandmamma and the wolf. The pot all ready. Never for years had she felt such blind unreasoning panic.

Then her intelligence reasserted itself. It was just some tramp, sleeping rough, living off the land.

Except that they weren't somehow sleeping rough. There was a dreadful organization and efficiency about it that frightened her. More like some campaigner living off enemy land. Besides, she told herself in excuse for her sudden hurried flight from the hollow, she had all the time, as she struggled upwards, this dreadful certainty that somewhere, someone was watching her.


'Rowena has found a mysterious stranger sojourning in our woods,' Gordon Greville said to fill an uncomfortable pause in the supper conversation. Too late, a distant anguish, he saw his youngest daughter flush, and knew that he had said the wrong thing yet again.

'Bully for her!' Ginny, elegant in low-cut dance dress and long earrings, took a sip of her Spanish Chablis (for this was an occasion) and shuddered. 'I should hang on to him, Wen. For dear life.'

Rowena remained silent. She chewed a piece of roast lamb as if waiting to swallow it before making a devastating retort. She wished now that in her first rush of uneasiness she had not confided in her father. Undevious himself, weak as water, he was the world's worst confidant. Besides, during the last week the wood and its occupant had lost their terror. Had acquired instead a mysterious and romantic quality. Each day she had found the stranger's bed. Tended, used, but always un-occupied. Each day she had felt his presence, sensed that he watched and waited behind some screen of leaves. Perhaps to see if she were friend or foe.

Three days ago, as a gesture of friendship, she had taken down a can of corned beef and a tin of beans. The following day the cans were there, empty, put neatly where the rabbit skin had been. She had been considering putting the remnants of this supper in a plastic bag to take down before school in the morning.

'I must say I don't relish the idea of someone living in our wood,' Mary Greville said, feeling it was up to her to protest, though about what she didn't quite know. Some sixth sense of danger perhaps. A feeling that just very slightly the world as she knew it was going even further askew. She glanced around in the silence to see if everyone had finished, and then held out her hand for their plates.

It was what Rowena called supper *en* extended *famille*. Eleanor was home. Rather larger than she should have been at four and a half months. But looking oddly young and touching in a blue cotton maternity dress with white collar and cuffs. Her husband, Bill Waterhouse, was very much in attend-ance. He had just counted out her vitamin pills, which he carried in the pocket of his shirt. Eleanor had written that hers was a check-list pregnancy with charts of what she should be eating or drinking or what exercises she should be doing at any given time. It must be good to be fussed and cherished and even ordered around like that.

'Shame on you, Mary,' Gordon said in his sandy rallying voice that rasped her nerves. 'With all the land we have.'

He watched his wife avert her eyes and the irritated colour come up under her still young-looking skin. Time was when those hazel eyes had looked at him in melting admiration. When every act of hers had sought to please him. She had, he had known now for many years, fallen in love with an entirely different man. The man she thought he was. The first man, as it were, in any sort of authority over her. Bright, eighteen, straight from a nice girls' school to University. To sit at the feet of youngish Professor Greville. A conscientious objector – it was his secret shame that he had risen while better men died. On him had been projected all her longings and yearnings. She had in her own way invented him. Given his pacifism a heroic quality which even he did not aspire to. Endowed him with qualities that the years had shown him not to possess.

That he loved her exactly as she was, he had never any doubt. Equally, he had no doubt that she no longer loved him. That was the hollow in the shell of their outwardly satisfactory family life. The skeleton in the cupboard. The basic nothingness that the family recognized without being able to put into words.

Mary had taken him with enthusiasm to her bosom and her bed and found him wanting. And so by some mysterious genetic law it followed that they all found him wanting too.

'Why shouldn't some outdoor-loving soul make his temporary habitat there?' Gordon Greville asked, nodding reassuringly at his pilot son-in-law who was frowning, very red in the face and sweaty with husbandly anxiety.

'Make his simple bed out of . . . what did you say it was, Rowena?'

'Bracken.'

'Well there! He's not robbing us of anything we need. Far healthier, I should think, than wire springs and foam rubber.'

'He had a fire,' Mary said sternly, handing out portions of

her lemon meringue pie, pursing her lips the way she hated doing, but which life with Gordon somehow made inevitable. She who in her youth had expected devoted love and warmth and protection now had to be the tough organizing one of the family. The years had changed her into a brisk competent middle-aged woman. Soon she would be a stringy-necked harridan – when really all her life she had yearned to be frivolous, indolent, cared for like Ginny.

'We're not short of kindling, Mary.'

'He might set the woods on fire.'

'They're too green to catch alight, *mamma mia*,' Rowena said didactically, watching beefy Brother-in-Law display the symptoms of robin-like territorial outrage, so lacking in her father. 'Besides, whoever it is had it all very carefully confined.'

'Who do *you* think it is?' Bill asked, looking aggressively from one to the other, his thick neck crested up like a stallion's.

'Eleanor's lover,' Rowena said promptly, 'Without doubt.'

'Seriously,' Bill asked sharply.

'Some old tramp,' Mr Greville suggested vaguely.

'I'm sure he's not old,' Rowena protested.

'Gypsies then.'

'Mmm.' Brother-in-Law mopped his forehead with a snowy handkerchief. 'Rum lot, gypsies.'

'They're all right if you treat them all right.'

'It's only one, and he isn't a gypsy.'

'Then it could be an impoverished student. Some enterprising chap working his way. Maybe around Europe. Living off the land. Sleeping rough.'

'But it didn't look rough at all. The bed, the fire . . .' Rowena's voice trailed.

'You know, green woods can still catch alight,' Ginny said, looking at her watch, and widening her lovely eyes. 'According to Simon . . .'

'Who the bloody hell is Simon?'

Only Brother-in-Law, the tough *hombre* pilot, winced at Rowena's language.

'Just someone I met, Wen.'

'Stop calling me that! Where? Where did you meet him?'

'None of your business.' Ginny began to stack the empty pudding plates. 'I certainly didn't trap him in the wood.'

'But him being the reason you're done up *comme ça*? Leaving nought, but nought, to the imagination?'

'He, darling,' Mr Greville said. 'He being the reason. You're getting somewhat careless with your syntax.'

'He's taking me to a dance, if that's what you mean, Wen.'

'Where?' Eleanor asked in pacifying tones.

'Walgrave Manor. The Farmers' Union Dinner.'

'Is he a farmer?' Bill asked hopefully.

'So it would seem.'

'Sound types, farmers.' It was First Officer Waterhouse's private fear that for fellow brothers-in-law he would acquire eventually some drug-taking drop-outs and Happy Hippies. And what with quick promotion from Second Officer, and now being on the crew of this royal flight from America, he was on his way up. CAVU – or in plain language, ceiling and visibility unlimited. Towards the rarified air of a captaincy in British Airways before he was forty.

'Shall we meet him, lovie?'

'I expect we'll be in a bit of a hurry, Mother. Anyway, you'll want to chat up Bill. Hear all about his royal trip.' She gave Brother-in-Law one of her sweet and dazzling and persuasive smiles. 'Queen's life in your hands, eh what, old boy?'

'Only on the eastbound.' Bill flushed with pleasure, modestly disclaiming.

'The westbound First Officer was years senior,' Eleanor said, her hand through her husband's arm proudly.

'Eleanor's biased. But they vetted us to the $n$th degree. And they've got maximum security on at Grantwick. Special passes. Every other maintenance worker a plain clothes detective.'

'Why Grantwick?' Mary Greville asked.

Bill finished off his pie, put his spoon neatly in the middle of his plate.

'That attack at Heathrow last month. Grantwick's not built up. Easier to contain.'

'They're surely not expecting anything against the Queen!' Gordon Greville said.

'Not really. But they have to take precautions. Three weeks before her trip, the top security men went to every place she's visiting in the States, organized everything with our own staff and the American police. The royal VC10 was withdrawn from service two days before the Queen left. Kept guarded in the main hangar. Every little piece checked. Even the tea ladies had to be positively vetted.'

'They had a good trip over,' Mary said.

'Piece of cake!'

'And when do you pick them up?'

'Sunday week. We go over as passengers tomorrow on the normal BA.505. Then we wait in New York for the Queen to return from Washington.'

'It's a great honour,' said Eleanor.

'And a great responsibility,' added her father.

Eleanor's hand tightened on her husband's arm. 'All possible precautions are taken.'

'Everything,' her husband agreed. 'Tabs are kept throughout the trip. The squawk ident is on the whole time, so the aircraft is always identified on the radar.'

'What is squawk ident?' Gordon enquired.

'IFF . . . Identification of Friendly Forces was what they called it in the war. A little transmitter on the VHF band that shows up big on the radar screen.'

'And I suppose special precautions are taken against bombs

on board?'

'Of course.'

'Is it in order to ask what?'

Bill Waterhouse looked mysterious. 'Well, not really supposed to say, but between these four walls and as we're all family and – '

' – since we've all been identified as Friendly Forces,' Ginny interrupted.

'Don't be so sure,' said Rowena. 'I can't hear Richard's little transmitter.'

' – it's really simply a safety precaution. They've got a special sniffer now. Smells out explosive yards away. No chance of a bomb. Not on this trip. No hi-jackers either.'

'Terrible business . . . this aircraft piracy.' Gordon Greville blinked behind his spectacles.

'Too right, it is.'

'Difficult to know what to do.'

'I know what to do.'

'What?' Rowena asked, knowing what was coming.

'Hang them,' Bill said.

Rowena watched her father wince.

'Or better still, kill them on board. Law of the sea.'

'Law of the jungle,' Mr Greville murmured sadly.

'We live in the jungle,' Ginny said with finality, walking towards the dining-room door. Outside the latticed windows, tyres swished on the drive. There was the sound of a powerful smooth-running engine. 'Well, I'm off. Look after yourself, Bill. We'll be thinking of you. Now, no peeping from upstairs, Wen!'

'As if I would,' Rowena returned beefy Brother-in-Law's wink with a frugal smile. 'It's Richard cœur-de-black-basalt who is the lad for that.'

'Bloody liar,' Richard uttered his first words.

'You know, you two wedded blissers,' Rowena said, 'a fearful thought has struck me. What if Eleanor is delivered of a bastard like Richard?'

'We'd be delighted.' Bill grinned hugely, though it was obvious that the horrendous possibility had not struck him before. 'A son first go off! Cigars all round on the flight deck!'

'A son like him though?' Rowena persisted.

'Nothing wrong with Richard.'

'That capital punishment wouldn't put right, you mean.' Rowena stood up, and carried the plates through into the kitchen.

'Don't take any notice, son.' Gordon Greville leaned forward. 'I used to get much worse tormenting in my youth.' He had told them often, though they never seemed interested. 'But it was my father. Imagine that! Colonel Greville. The army was his life. His mind went completely in the end . . .' He paused in his reminiscences. They were getting even less attention than usual. Richard wasn't even pretending to listen.

Beefy Brother-in-Law had waved him to Ginny's empty chair. 'Tell you what, Richard. I'll show you my revolver. Specially issued.'

Gordon Greville watched his son's eyes gleam with interest. He was a strange lad. He waited, almost hopefully for some sassy remark to be called through from Rowena in the kitchen. But none came.

As soon as the front door shut behind Ginny, Rowena had gone upstairs to the landing above the entrance porch. It had a tall slit of a coffin window that by day gave a long view down to the end of the drive. There were two gig lamps beside the entrance, clearly illuminating Ginny, her boy-friend, and a three-year-old MG Magnette.

Rowena told herself she was simply curious to see, sum up and acquire possible useful knowledge of this latest acquisition of Ginny's. The mantle of their rather uneasy, lumpy family life was upon her. She wanted nothing more than to score off Ginny. Ginny the lovely, somehow untouchable elder sister. The rival who always won, scratch her frustrations off like that.

She saw Ginny spotlit in the spill of the door lights, with a tallish, well-built man. In his late twenties maybe. Difficult to say. His face was upshadowed as he crossed the cone of the headlamps. Brown hair – not cut in any particular fashion. Thin, bony, smiling with restrained politeness.

The affair she decided hadn't got very far, or had gone too far, because they didn't kiss. Ginny seemed rather distant with him, but then she was the princess in the ivory tower and apt to be like that. He looked reasonably prosperous and astonishingly sane.

He made some remark about the fineness of the night, opened the door for Ginny and tucked her inside. The car turned and disappeared in a wash of thrown-up gravel chippings, its headlights leaping ahead till they fingered the low hedge that lined the country lane and marked Fallowlands' boundary.

Its rear lights shrank. But before they altogether vanished, a figure detached itself from the clump of giant rhododendrons to the north of the house. It crossed the gravel, head down and crouched down on the drive, soft as a cat, disturbing not a pebble of its surface.

Then it, too, disappeared – in the direction of the stranger's wood.


The ringing of the front door bell caught Mary Greville in the act of doing something of which she was ashamed – watching television in the middle of a warm summer afternoon. Not even the excuse, which some of her friends used, that it was Wimbledon. She was on her own and she was watching the repeat news film of the royal departure for New York.

Gordon would have scorned her sentimentality, as he scorned her intermittent churchgoing, but it too still had the power to move her. A little flag waving, a little pomp and circumstance. The National Anthem played by the Scots Guards. Besides, the family had a stake in it. Basked at a distance in the reflected glory.

Bill Waterhouse had left yesterday on the positioning flight to bring back the royal aircraft. When the television cameras were at Grantwick next week again, his would be the face next to the head of the crew, being introduced first to her Majesty by the Captain, shaking the Queen's hand bowing low.

Bliss!

Mary was alone in the house. Eleanor had gone to Dr Mason, the Greville's family doctor, for a check-up (insisted upon by dear devoted Bill before he left). University term had finished, but Gordon was interviewing for next year's intake. Ginny was at her Art College. Rowena and Richard at school. Rowena was sitting her last A-level this afternoon – Biology. A dodgy subject for her – which meant she would be pretty short-tempered when she got home.

The front door bell rang again. Taking a last look at the Queen, waving at the top of the steps before going inside the British Airways VC10, Mary Greville switched off the set, walked across the hall and opened the door.

On the step stood a slim, dark-haired, dark-eyed young man, wearing an open-necked cotton shirt and jeans with a leather folder tucked under his arm. Good-looking in a swarthy way. Behind him, parked in the circular sweep of the drive, a grey Land-Rover.

The young man smiled engagingly showing very white, very regular teeth, stretched out his hand, 'You must be Mrs Greville?'

Mary Greville nodded, shook hands briefly, almost answered, 'And you must be Simon?' but paraphrased it to 'Are you a friend of Ginny's?'

The young man shook his head, laughed, spread his hands.

He had a charming laugh. A deep throaty voice. 'I'm sure I wish I were, Mrs Greville. But I'm afraid, you won't know me.'

There was just a touch of a foreign accent, disarmingly attractive. Mary smiled vaguely and waited.

'I hope I didn't drag you in from your lovely garden.' He paused for a moment, his eyes travelling round the front part of the lawn. 'And I am sorry to make so much noise and dust turning my Land-Rover round.' He gave an apologetic shrug and smile. 'But it is difficult to turn.'

'It *is* difficult,' Mary said. 'The drive is so narrow. We've been meaning to make a turning circle for years. But in any case, I didn't know you were here till I heard the bell.'

'You are so very isolated. But that is part of the beauty.'
Mary nodded.

'The fact is, Mrs Greville . . .' His eyes came back to her face. 'Oh, my name by the way is Shaw. John Shaw. I run a photographic firm. And we've been taking some rather nice pictures in this area.'

'I see,' Mary answered noncommitally. A salesman. She wondered how on earth she could decently get rid of him without spending anything. Usually she tried to buy a small item from whatever itinerant salesmen happened their way. But these days everything was so expensive and a professor's pay was so small.

'May I show you one of them?' He held his head on one side in an exaggerated un-English gesture of supplication.

'If you wish.'

He raised his brows in mock sadness at her unenthusiastic tone. Then with a quick bright smile and a conjurer's wave of thin sun-burned hands, produced the folder from under his arm and extracted a ten by seven photograph, which he handed to her. He stepped back a pace and carefully watched her expression.

'Oh,' Mary exclaimed despite herself. 'Why, it's Fallowlands! From the air! How marvellous! It looks simply super! How did you get that?'

'Quite easily. We hire an aircraft. From Biggin Hill. Good, isn't it?' He came and stood beside her on the top step, peering over her shoulder admiring it with her. 'But then, it's a lovely house. Quite unique.'

'We like it. But you've got it in such detail. You must have come awfully low.'

'We did rather. You didn't notice us?'

'No. But then we get used to the aircraft all the time. We're right on the landing path to the main runway at Grantwick. Oh, they've given us sound-proofing. But it's a great pity.'

He shrugged, lost interest in the problem of Fallowlands, stared up at her expectantly.

'How much is it?' Mary asked, holding the photograph against her chest. She had already decided if it were at all possible she must have it. She would give it to Eleanor and Bill as a present for their second wedding anniversary next month. It could sit on the sitting-room mantelpiece beside the signed royal photograph which the crew were always presented with.

The young man laughed at her eagerness. He waved his hands disclaimingly like some Arab in the market place. 'Ah, you like that, but you have not yet seen the finished article. We enlarge the one you have there and hand colour it in the exact shades of your beautiful house and garden. The result is . . .' He kissed his fingers. 'Perfection!'

'Can't I just buy *this*?'

'Alas no, Mrs Greville! It would just not be worth our while. But we would very soon do the work. My partner works skilfully but fast! And if you ever wanted to sell the house, which heaven forbid, what better to have?'

'The price?'

The young man spread his hands, smiled apologetically, 'Not very much. Forty.'

'Pounds?'

He nodded.

Mary drew in her breath sharply. 'Oh, I couldn't. Really, I'm sorry . . .' She stretched her hand out, proffering the picture towards him.

He didn't take it. He folded his arms over his chest, held his head on one side, frowning down thoughtfully at his shoes. 'I do so want you to have it, Mrs Greville.'

'So do I. But . . .'

'I tell you what I do.' He snapped his fingers in sudden inspiration. 'My partner may object, but never mind. Because it is such an attractive house, so very beautiful picture, I will put it in for *half* price, if you allow us to use it to show other customers. Yes?'

Mary hesitated fractionally. 'That's very generous of you.'

'My pleasure.'

'All right then.'

'And now, Mrs Greville, may I write down your order somewhere? My knees are too thin to write it on properly.'

He laughed. It suddenly seemed discourteous that she had not already invited him inside.

'I'm so sorry. Yes, please do come in.' She stood back and ushered him into the cool shadowy hall. It smelled that day of Treece's wax and pink thornless roses. The strange young man drew in a deep breath almost too deep for pure aesthetic pleasure. Almost, Mary thought sentimentally, feeling vaguely maternal, as if he had been on a long journey and had at last stepped over the threshold of home.

'Home?' the young man smiled regretfully, and in answer repeated her own question back to her. 'Where is my home? That is difficult exactly to say.'

They were sitting on the patio outside the dining-room and Mary had made tea, after their tour of the house and garden.

He had needed to look carefully around the garden and the exterior to get exactly the right shades for the colour tinting. But he had also been very interested in the inside too. He had seemed so obsessed, enchanted and delighted with the whole place. 'A dream house,' he had called it. His rapture had kindled hers, half stifled by the hours it took to clean with only a half day's help from Mrs Bristowe. Mr Shaw had lavishly praised her colour schemes, her hand-made cushions and curtains and admired with unfeigned interest the various views from all the little windows.

He found the history of the house intriguing – the mullioned Tudor windows, the cool dark cellar that had been used to store wine, tobacco and spices smuggled in from France. Rowena's room with its flowered wallpaper and chintz curtains and its french doors on to the balcony particularly appealed to him.

'Beautiful!' he said, standing beside her on the balcony looking all round at the panorama of thick green leaves without another house to be seen. 'What privacy, Mrs Greville!'

'Except . . .!' Mary Greville pointed up into the blue sky to where a glittering silver Pan-American Jumbo was approaching from the east.

The whistle of the jets changed to a scream. Mary Greville covered her ears with her hands. Momentarily the sun went out as the 747 passed only four or five hundred feet above them, directly overhead.

Mr Shaw laughed. 'There is always a fly in every ointment, dear Mrs Greville. And at least for going on holiday it is convenient to be near the airport.'

So enthusiastic had he been that she had even half expected that he was going to ask to rent the house from her when they did go away, and a refusal hovered unnecessarily on her lips.

Back downstairs, he had studied with professional interest the photographs on the piano in the sitting-room and on the desk in Gordon's den. And she had decided that he was probably a lonely rootless young man attracted by the vision of an apparently happy family in a gracious old house. Yet there was nothing soft and sentimental in the face that smiled so quickly and easily. The nose was thin and sharp. The lips hardly ever still, never in repose, as if not to let you catch them.

In the garden, she had changed her mind. Decided he was simply determined to make a go of his job. Carefully and conscientiously as they strolled around the gravel paths he had noted the colours of the bricks and the wall tiles and the darker, moss-clumped tiles of the steep pitched roof, the silvering of the old oak window-frames and the pointing of Tudor stone at the cornices.

'It's a pity about the telephone wires,' she had remarked, seeing him note them.

'Artistically *unforgiveable*, Mrs Greville. But I expect you are very glad to have it. You are so isolated here. I don't suppose you have many visitors?'

'No. You see, Gordon, my husband, studies a great deal. He likes to be quiet.'

'Very naturally.'

'A few tradesmen call. The milkman, and the baker used to call. But not now.'

'You could be self-sufficient almost?'

'Oh, we grow a good deal.' She had pointed out the vegetable garden, and the apple and the plum trees. Over the exact shades of the flowers in the rear part of the garden, he had asked her opinion. That wonderful yellow of the laburnum arch. Too bright for sienna, too vivid for primrose. The red of the geraniums seemed to vibrate and pulse into orange in the unclouded heat of the afternoon sun, and then back again to a bitter angry red. Orange or red? He had made the decision sound momentous and important. She had chosen, with a vague feeling of unease, the bitter red.

'Home,' he said again lightly, and sipped his tea, 'is now for me, as you English say, where I hang my hat.'

'You're not English?'

'Alas, no. My father was a surgeon in Teheran. He died, alas. My mother French. The last time I heard from her she was in Beirut.'

'You're not a close family?'

'No.'

Mary Greville nodded. She felt guiltily that she had talked too much about her own family to him. Their problem with Richard, their aspirations for Rowena. She hadn't meant to be a bore. And he seemed genuinely interested. Now, however, she felt it was his turn. But the young man offered no further information. He drank his tea, his eyes fixed on the old walls musingly, at the tiny grille of the old cellar window, just visible above the lily-of-the-valley bed, as if wondering how to capture the varying colours of them all.

'Are you married?'

He shook his head, drew the corners of his mouth down with exaggerated regret. 'Again, alas, no! I have not enough money. Marriage necessitates a home, yes? I would like one such as this.' He waved his hand to encompass the creeper-hung walls, the garden, the distant woods. 'But I am not so lucky, or perhaps not so deserving as your fortunate husband.'

'You'll soon work your business up,' Mary murmured vaguely, turning her wrist round so that she could look at her watch. Four-thirty. Eleanor would be back any time now. So would Rowena. Resentful that her tea wasn't ready and her mother was entertaining a stranger. Scornful perhaps of that amount of money to be spent on a quite unnecessary photograph.

'Yes, of course,' the young man said, 'soon we shall, as you say, work up our business. Given a little luck, time is on our side, yes?' Yet his smile for the first time had a savage edge to it that she didn't like. As if he sensed that she wanted to get rid of him and that he didn't intend to go. She wished she'd never seen him or his photograph, for that matter. She felt a chill crawl up her bare arms, despite the summer heat.

But the next moment she was sure she was mistaken. He smiled at her warmly. 'And now I have taken up enough of your time, Mrs Greville.' He stood up. He followed her into the hall, commenting now on the fine old brick porch.

'The swallows used to nest above that window.' She pointed at a jumble of twigs and mess. 'But not this year.'

She remembered that she had been vaguely disappointed (for it is a country superstition that no harm comes where swallows nest) that none had returned to Fallowlands. Then, ushering him towards his car, she smiled briskly, 'Just as well. They're messy creatures.'

'But if I am not mistaken – ' he shaded his eyes – 'one of your own brood is returning, yes?'

A small figure no bigger than someone at the wrong end of a telescope had begun to come down the long drive from the road. Its pace was disconsolate. Its feet were scuffing up little puffs of dust.

Rowena in another of her adolescent furies.

'I'm going to keep the photograph as a surprise,' Mary Greville said suddenly, in case she didn't get rid of him before Rowena arrived.

'Of course. Present them with the *fait accompli*.' He smiled broadly. 'I promise we shall deliver in two days' time.'

Yet it didn't sound like a promise, Mary thought. It sounded like a threat. She watched Rowena's slow approach.

Now for some reason, she no longer looked like someone at the wrong end of a telescope. More a figure sighted down the barrel of a rifle. Then, as the stranger's Land-Rover accelerated down the drive towards Rowena, she was possesed by a sudden terror, as if she half expected to see him aim the vehicle deliberately at her daughter. She closed her eyes, and when she opened them again, he had already passed Rowena in a flurry of dust.

The girl turned and shouted something angrily at him.

Mary stood for a moment with her hand resting for support on the warm bricks of the house wall. Her cotton dress clung to her back, but she shivered. Her forehead was clammy with a cold sweat, as if she had been infected by some swift illness. She had a sudden desire, unusual for her because she was determinedly unpossessive, to gather the family safely within the security of the home. She wished Eleanor would return, that Richard's bus would come, that Ginny wasn't going straight from Art College to meet this latest boy-friend.

Then the feeling – perhaps it had been physical, after all – disappeared as suddenly as it had come. Frowning at herself, Mary Greville went inside, tidied away the stranger's cup and saucer, switched on the kettle in the kitchen to make Rowena's tea.

The next day deteriorated as suddenly as the weather. Typical British summer holiday stuff. Wakes week in Bolton, according to the radio. Second day at Lord's. Deceivingly bright in the morning, not a cloud in the sky. All the girls in their summer dresses. Heavy continuous rain by the time Ginny pushed open the door of the Surrey Yeoman, their local in Medbridge. But that wasn't all by a long chalk.

To begin with she was hellishly and unforgiveably late, Simon was already propping up the bar, his eyes fixed on the streaming windows, frowning. She couldn't decide whether he was worrying about the effect of the downpour on his first hay cut, or about her. She decided before he spoke that it was the hay.

'Thought you were going to be early?' he remarked equably enough by way of greeting. He raised his thick brows ironically. He was judging at the County Show in Horsham tomorrow, besides entering a couple of his own stock, so he had to be up at the crack of dawn. In all his doings Simon Fairfax was the kind of man who demanded cooperation from wind, weather and women. While she herself expected what? Not anything quite so old-fashioned as devotion, though something regrettably like it. Pursuit. Rowena used to say scornfully that Ginny was the princess in the ivory tower, the one who let her golden hair down for the prince to climb up, though frankly she doubted if Ginny would bestir herself to do that. Certainly the more attractive Ginny found a man, by some ultra-feminine quirk, the more cool and casual did she become.

'So I was.' She climbed on to the stool Simon drew out for her, pulled off her scarf and freed her long fair hair with a shake of her head. 'I was held up.'

'That much I gathered.'

'Budgen . . . he's our Art Tutor . . . would keep going on and on.' She broke off suddenly, wondering if she should tell him the real reason she'd been late. But she'd known Simon for such a short time. And if he was attracted to her at all it was to the surface sophisticated Ginny. Not the kind of girl who panicked like some Victorian Miss because she'd been followed by a stranger.

'Did he make you miss your usual train?' Simon asked, his grey eyes fixed on her face in mild puzzlement.

'Who?'

'Your tutor. What was he called? Some helluva name?'

'Budgen. Oh, yes.' She nodded vigorously. 'He did. I had to catch the six-thirty-five. It was chokker.'

'Blast Budgen,' Simon said mildly, his eyes crinkling up.

She nodded. Though of course it hadn't been Budgen. It had been the strange man who'd followed her. Or whom she thought had been following her.

While Simon rang the polished brass bell marked service, Ginny glanced around the almost empty room. An elderly man who ran the old-fashioned pharmacy in the High Street was sitting with his wife at a table by the window studying the bar supper menu. Two men were playing darts at the far end. Locals by the look of them, but no one she knew. No sign of the man who'd been following her.

She frowned, trying to give herself a description of him. Medium height. She measured Simon's work-toughened frame with her eyes. A good five inches shorter than Simon, she would say.

Simon turned suddenly and smiled down at her, his expression quizzical. 'Something about me bothering you?'

She smiled. 'Only slightly. Why?'

'Pity.' His tone became less teasing. 'Because a good deal about you bothers *me*.'

'Actually,' she said, 'I was just wondering how tall you are?'

He laughed. 'You never fail to surprise me. How tall am I? Haven't a clue. Yes, I have. Six foot plus. Why?'

'Just wondering.'

Arthur the barman came through rubbing his hands on his apron. 'Sorry for the delay, sir. Been tapping a new barrel. 'Evening, miss. Can't say it's a good one, eh?'

'Frightful.'

'Same as usual, is it, Guinevere?' Simon asked.

He was the only person who insisted on calling her by her real name. Her father used to when she was small. But somehow the family had scorned him out of it.

'Yes, please.' She nodded abstractedly.

Simon shot her a keen glance which she didn't notice. She had been thinking that the man had been more Arthur's height. But slighter built and younger. Moving very swiftly and softly on his feet.

'And shall you be supping with us tonight, eh, sir?'

'That was the general idea.'

'Well, there's a grilled trout. That I can really recommend. Fisherman friend of mine brought them in this morning. That suit you?'

'Fine,' Ginny said.

'Or there's tame rabbit pie. Never serve the wild, never.

Not since the mixy. I had a queer-looking herbert at my door yesterday offering me a dozen. Sent him away with a flea in his ear. Probably poached them from your place, miss. You'd never know.'

'No, we wouldn't,' Ginny agreed, wishing she could shake away this odd feeling of something rather awful closing in on her. Of normal life going on all about her, and yet something not normal going on underneath.

'So it's the same for you, is it, sir? And how about a little wine to wash it down?' He handed Simon the plastic-covered wine list.

'Guinevere, any preference?'

'Just whatever you like.'

Simon looked at her over the top of the list. 'You're very compliant this evening.'

'Is that unusual?'

'Very.'

'I thought you liked your women compliant.' She smiled mockingly.

'I like my women,' he said slowly, putting down the wine list, 'like you.' He rested his hand lightly on her shoulder. 'Except not in the plural. I could only cope with one.' His fingers lightly brushed her neck. She shivered. The pleasure of the moment passed.

It had been the touch of the man's newspaper on the back of her neck that had so panicked her. Silly really, bloody silly. He had been such a nondescript-looking man. One of the crowd. Wearing an ordinary-looking fawn suit, and a light brown trilby hat.

Large sunglasses with side-pieces. And why not? The morning had started out sunny. She had been wearing, still was for that matter, a sleeveless cotton dress. She'd first noticed the man on the 8.09 Medbridge to East Croydon train. Just past Warlingham he'd come down peering in the compartments as if looking for a vacant seat. There wasn't one so he'd stood outside in the corridor, reading the *Telegraph,* and from time to time glancing in.

By odd coincidence he'd caught the same 45 bus as she had from outside East Croydon station and alighted immediately behind her at the Felsden Art College stop. Then he'd vanished.

But in the afternoon when the maligned Mr Budgen had punctually finished his tutorial, she'd spotted him from the top of the college steps. The man in the fawn suit leaning up against the bus standard, reading an evening paper. She dawdled. A 45 bus went by. The man remained.

Even so, it all still seemed fairly harmless. She refused to allow herself to let another bus go. She was meeting Simon and he'd asked her to be early. In the first place this man, this odd little man, probably wasn't following her at all. And in the second, she was by no means unused to attention. She knew she was pretty. Beautiful even, according to some people. Men often tried to make her acquaintance. Any time now, she thought, sauntering to the bus stop and joining the queue, he would advance, raise that silly hat, and make some excuse about their having met before, 'Didn't she remember?'

Instead, he sat directly behind her on the bus. Though he made no sound, she was as physically aware of him as she was of Simon. Yet in a totally opposite way. The man in the fawn suit's nearness chilled her to the marrow of her bones. She could feel his malevolence. As if in broad daylight he might suddenly lean forward and put his hands round her throat, before anyone had time to stop him. Odd, silly, strange, maybe, but that was when this feeling had begun. That underneath and within this normal British summer day, behind the cricket scores and the Wimbledon matches, schools breaking up and holidays beginning, something terrible was about to close in.

Then as the fawn-suited man had spread open his paper, the pages had brushed the back of her neck, parted her hair like fingers. She had suddenly panicked. Just as the bus pulled clear from a stop, she got to her feet, rushed down the aisle, on to the platform, and leapt off the moving bus.

Her feet jarred, but she didn't fall. She heard the conductor yell. She had a glimpse of the man in the fawn suit standing up, his glasses turned in her direction. Then his diminished figure on the platform gesticulating to the conductor. The ping, ping, ping of the conductor's sharply rung bell, and the big bus slowed urgently.

As the fawn-suited man jumped from it, Ginny cast around for somewhere to go. Now she was sure of his malevolence. It was as if he wasn't now so much following her as stalking her.

Behind her was a meagre row of shops. A greengrocer's, a turf accountant. Then beyond them, blessedly, the ugly Victorian edifice of the Public Baths. Thankfully she hurried inside down the lavatory-tiled corridor, scrabbled in her bag for a coin, paid at the kiosk, waited interminably while the woman asked her suspiciously if she wanted to hire a towel, and got her ticket. As she followed the arrow marked *Females,* she saw the figure of the fawn-suited man silhouetted in the entrance doorway.

She was reasonably sure he hadn't seen her. But he would only have to ask the woman in the ticket kiosk. Ginny sat in the changing cubicle for fifteen minutes. The damp wooden slats dug into her thighs. The place smelled of chlorine and feet, echoed to the amplified screams and whale-like wallowings beyond the glass doors.

At six-thirty she decided that she could wait no longer. She crept out of the changing-room. The ticket kiosk was closed. There was no one to tell the fawn-suited man that she had gone. The corridor was empty. The street busy. But no fawn-suited man at the bus stop or anywhere in sight. All the same she didn't risk waiting. She walked the rest of the mile and a half to East Croydon station and caught the seven-ten to Medbridge.

38

Just before the whistle went, the fawn-suited man rushed out of the down platform buffet bar and into the same compartment. He stood so close to where she sat that the toe of his brown shoe almost touched hers. She watched it fascinated, wondering, hoping even, that it would slide closer and nudge her. But it didn't. Not even in the tunnel. He never looked up from his paper. He still wore the dark glasses. He never turned the pages.

He got out at Medbridge. She heard those brown shoes echo over the metal footbridge close behind her. A fawn-sleeved arm stretched alongside hers to proffer his ticket at the barrier. Then she lost him in the rush for the car park. It had begun to rain. Everyone fled away as shapeless and formless as drab autumn leaves in the wind. He was nowhere in sight when she reached the Surrey Yeoman.

'Well, cheers,' Simon said, lifting his tankard, nodded towards her frosty drink. 'Drink it up while it's fizzy, there's a good girl! You're already one behind.'

'Cheers! And good luck for tomorrow.'

'Thanks,' Simon raised his glass. 'Of course you could always come along and bring me it in person.'

'Luck? Do you think I would?'

'I reckon so. And even if you didn't it would be nice to have you.'

'I am quite overcome. But really I ought to go into College.'

'Budgen would miss you, would he?' Simon smiled.

'Not Budgen, no.' But the man in the fawn suit perhaps. In silence she watched Arthur carefully put down in front of them the hot platters of grilled trout, crisp with almonds and swimming in butter. Maybe the man in the fawn suit would be waiting somewhere on the 8.09 from Medbridge, searching the train, then waiting for the 45 bus, getting off at the Felsden Art College. Then waiting again for her return. If he was, should she go up and ask him what the hell he was doing?

She stared at the reflection of the wet windows in the mirror behind the bar, trying to imagine what the man would say, what excuse he would give. Whether he would stand his ground or turn tail.

'Six sharp, if you're coming?' Simon said, passing her the salt.

She picked up her fork. 'Six,' she gave a theatrical shudder that was not altogether assumed. 'The mind boggles.' She stared fascinated into the mirror. A man was passing along the High Street outside, thin shoulders hunched, hat drawn down over his ears. Medium height, nondescript. Could have been anyone. The hat was a large trilby. Fawn. The mac looked fawn. He wore glasses. Dark. She couldn't be sure. Might have been the same man but she couldn't be sure of that either.

'So you're not coming?' Simon said watching her expression closely.

'No.'

'Someone you've got to see tomorrow?' There was a tightness about his mouth that she both applauded and mourned.

'Not really.' She dug her fork into her fish. 'Just something that I've simply got to find out.'


There was a fitful moonlight by the time Gordon Greville arrived home and slipped his key into the Yale latch of Fallowlands' front door.

'That you, dear?' Mary called from the kitchen, her tone edged with surprise. 'I thought you were coming on the last train. You didn't want me to keep supper, did you?'

She emerged, smiling with determined brightness as she always did for his return, then presented her somehow nerveless cheek for his quick cold kiss.

'No, thank you, my dear, I had a bite at my desk.'

He saw his wife register what she would call his pomposity.

'Anyway,' he said cheerily, advancing towards the empty hearth rubbing his hands as if it contained a blazing fire, 'nice to get everything finished and not have to go into college for umpteen weeks.'

'Super,' Mary said unenthusiastically. She found Gordon's presence in the house during the long summer vacation a nuisance. His self-important disappearance to his study after breakfast, his insistence on quiet in the house while ignoring the godawful noise of the aircraft up above. His objection to Mrs Bristowe using the vacuum-cleaner while he prepared next year's lectures or his endless text-book on the Liberal Revival. 'I've cut some sandwiches,' Mary said, 'I thought I'd make a milk drink when Ginny comes in.'

'She won't be long. I saw her and that farmer fellow getting into his car just as I passed the Surrey Yeoman. Looks a nice chap.'

He saw Mary smile in the way that said clearer than words, 'All people seem nice chaps to you.' But not tenderly as she *used* to say it.

'Where are the others?' Gordon asked her.

'Eleanor's in bed. She gets so tired these evenings.' She spoke anxiously.

'I remember you got tired when you were expecting the kids,' he said gently, reaching out to put his arm round her shoulders, but she stood too far away and too rigidly for him to reach her.

'But *I* had to work. Teaching three days a week. On Bill's salary she's got nothing to do but put her feet up all day.'

'She's probably missing Bill.'

'Oh,' Mary's face broke into a smile, 'she had a phone call from him this afternoon. Yes, from Washington. It was clear as a bell. Clearer than us to the corner stores,' she said. 'She was *so* thrilled.'

'He'd got there safely then!'

'Dead on schedule. Very chuffed with it all. But missing

Eleanor. Flags out everywhere for the Queen. Marvellous reception apparently. And, of course, they're being made a great fuss of too. Bill and his crew. He's been filmed for TV over there. Wined and dined.' She stared into the empty hearth vicariously enjoying her daughter's pride in her husband. For some reason he felt a stab of unnatural anger and resentment.

'Rowena?'

She replied carelessly. 'Upstairs reading.'

'And Richard?' he asked after a moment as her expression remained abstracted and withdrawn.

'Oh, Richard.' She exclaimed, her attention jolted back. 'Yes, Richard.' Her well-shaped lips tightened. 'You'll have to speak to him. Really he's beyond a joke. Getting to be a real lout. His school report is absolutely terrible. And this afternoon . . . you know how silly-sensitive Rowena is . . . well, he brought in a half-dead hare just as she got back from school.'

'Why did he do that?'

'Said that was how he found it. But Rowena said he'd done it himself.'

'I can't believe that,' Gordon murmured without conviction.

'Wait. That's not all. Before Rowena could bring herself to look at the poor thing, he got hold of my rolling pin, and . . .'

Mary lifted her hand and brought it down sharply in a gesture more expressive than words.

'Finished it off?'

'Like that.' Mary snapped her fingers.

They stared at one another for a moment in silence. Perhaps, Gordon thought, the household was all too female orientated and dominated. But somehow no one, not even Mary who *should* have doted on her only son, seemed to understand Richard. As a young boy, of course, she had spoiled him. But not now.

'He's at a difficult age,' he murmured feebly. 'Most boys have a cruel streak.'

Then she looked at him wide-eyed, as if saying, 'But you haven't,' despising him even for that. She shrugged. 'But you'll speak to him?'

'Of course. I'll go up now and have a bath, and have a word with young Richard on my way.'

'What about your hot drink and sandwiches?' she asked in a sudden guilty tone, as if mindful that she was treating him as less than the rightful family head.

'I'll have them in my dressing-gown,' he said more genially than he felt. 'Might as well wait till we're all in.'

The sentence and the sentiment had a cosy family ring. All safe and sound under the old roof. He climbed the ancient treads of the stairs slowly, hoping that Richard would be asleep, and his beastliness at least pushed further to the back of their minds by tomorrow.

He tapped on Rowena's door, 'Good night, my dear.'

Her voice replied with exaggerated sleepiness designed to repel him. ' 'Night.'

'Like some Horlicks and a bite?'

'Thanks, no. Slimming.'

'Good night then, my dear.'

A long, long yawn. ' 'Night.'

Before he tapped on Richard's door, he listened. He heard the sound of deep breathing. Quietly he turned the handle. His son lay on his side, one hand tucked under his cheek, the other lying gracefully over the rumpled bed cover. It was difficult to imagine that square supple hand executing the beastliness that Mary had reported to him. The young face flushed with sleep was wiped of its habitual scowl, the expression of the narrow eyes hidden under innocent thick-fringed lids, the mouth slightly open in pious supplication.

He stirred a little in the fan of light from the landing, and softly Gordon Greville tiptoed out and closed the door. He had just run his bath when he heard Ginny come in, and her voice calling to her mother across the hall.

He bathed hastily, put on his pyjamas and dressing-gown so as not to keep his womenfolk waiting. And he had just greeted Ginny when the front door bell rang.

# dead
# overhead

'Who could that be? Simon?'

Mary glanced questioningly at Ginny as the door bell pealed again. Ginny was lying on the sofa with her shoes kicked off, staring up at the raftered ceiling.

'I'd doubt it.' Ginny shrugged. 'He'll be half way home by now.' But she smiled as if she half hoped it might be, swung her legs down, shoved her slim feet into their high-heeled shoes, and tossing her hair behind her shoulders clipped smartly across the polished boards of the hall floor.

Gordon Greville hesitated. Then, intercepting a look of flustered exasperation directed at his threadbare dressing-gown, with which he refused to part, remained seated where he was, and busied himself in a book.

Mary stood up, prepared to welcome and inspect Ginny's latest boy-friend. From across the hall she heard Ginny's voice, puzzled but quite friendly. And then Ginny was calling over her shoulder, 'Someone for you, Mother.'

She came back into the sitting-room, leaving the front door ajar. A whisper of cool night air drifted in. It smelled of white jasmine and nicotiana, and sodden earth. A sweet mixture but funereal and sad.

'Who is it? Why didn't you ask them in?'

'It's not a *social* call, Mother.'

'What is it then?'

'They're delivering something.'

'Oh, Lord.' Mary put her hand to her mouth. What on earth would Gordon say about her extravagance? She glanced in his direction, but he was apparently absorbed in *The Life of Campbell Bannerman*.

'Go on, Mother.' Ginny gave her a gentle push.

Damn, Mary thought, walking across the hall. She would have to give them a cheque immediately. She only hoped her housekeeping account would stand it.

'Good evening, Mrs Greville.' It was, as she feared, the dark-haired young photographer who stood in the cone of light from the porch lantern. The same grey Land-Rover was just distinguishable parked in the shadow of the rhodo-dendron spinney. 'I have – ' the young man's very white smile waved in the darkness like a flag of peace – 'a very nice surprise for you.' His voice was half apologetic, half self-congratulatory. 'It is perhaps a little late.' And before Mary had time to agree: 'But not too late, I think, for a very nice surprise.'

'Five past eleven.'

The photographer thrust out his wrist and looked at his watch. 'So it is. We were in the district making a delivery. So we thought to give you this very nice surprise.'

'Thanks,' Mary said flatly.

'It is all ready.' His dark eyes searched her face, disappointed at her lack of enthusiasm. 'Our motto is, better a day early than a day late. Yes?'

'Of course.'

'So we may bring it in. My colleague and I? Put it carefully somewhere? It is framed. It is glass. It is *precious*.'

Mary advanced on to the top step and drew the front door almost shut behind her. 'I haven't told my husband yet,' she said in a low urgent voice. 'The cost, you see.'

'But when we bring it in, we will not tell him what it cost. Nor do you need to pay now.'

'Who is it, Mary?' Gordon's voice came questioningly behind her. She heard his slippered feet approaching.

'There.' The young man smiled. 'You go and make peace with your good husband. I will get the picture from the Land-Rover and we shall presently bring it in.' Just before he left the cone of light, he said, 'And don't worry, it is well wrapped, if you want to keep it as a birthday surprise.'

She nodded and turned. Gordon stood under the big oak beam that divided the sitting-room from the hall. 'Who on earth was that?'

'People delivering something.'

'What, dear?' And reproachfully, 'Something for the house?'

'No . . . it's . . . well, a present.'

Perhaps because of her hesitation, he assumed that the present was for him. His sallow skin actually coloured boyishly. He looked quite moved. He dipped his nose embarrassedly in his drink and murmured 'You shouldn't have done that, really.' Not as a reproach, but the way people do when they're pleased.

'Are we going to be allowed to see it?' he asked when the door remained open but nothing and no one appeared.

Ginny sighed, 'What the hell have you been buying, O foolish mother of four?' She gathered up her bag and scarf.

'Well, I'm off to bed. It's some hunk of junk she's bid for at an auction,' she said to her father. 'Full of dry rot and death watch.'

She was almost at the top of the stairs when the young man came in. He stood for a moment following her with his eyes, absent-mindedly snapping his fingers for two men to follow him in, making heavy weather of carrying between them a flat rectangular cloth-covered parcel. Carefully they leaned it against the oak panelling of the hall, and then stood a pace behind the young man. The two newcomers glanced around with uninhibited interest.

'She is a very, very beautiful girl, your daughter, Mrs Greville. Very, as they say, special. But forgive me. I forget my manners. These are my two colleagues.' He indicated the hefty young man in jeans with clean-cropped red hair, and a slim dapper man in a fawn suit and trilby hat, incongruously wearing dark wrap-around sunglasses.

'Good evening,' Mary said.

'Good evening,' the fawn-suited man replied.

The red-haired man jerked his head, but said nothing.

'Forgive my colleagues. Neither of them understand much English. But they understand photography. They have an artist's eye, yes? They thought your house – ' he tapped the swaddled picture – 'so beautiful. I tell them inside it is even lovelier. They wished so very much to see it.'

'Splendid, splendid.' Gordon advanced, hand outstretched. Always the first to welcome a foreigner, always more than happy to display his lack of any sort of criticism. A smile of welcome spread over his face.

'My husband, Mr . . . er . . . er,' Mary racked her brains. 'Shaw.'

Gordon grasped the man's right hand, and shook it warmly.

'Come along in.' He beckoned them in, the red-haired giant had to duck his head under the beam. 'Tudor, you know,' he said to Shaw. 'Sit down.' He pointed to the cretonne-covered sofa. 'How about a drink?' He smiled. 'It isn't every day people bring me a present. We were just having Horlicks. But how about coffee? Or something stronger?'

Mr Shaw hesitated politely, and then opted for coffee. If it wasn't too much trouble. It was. But it was worth it. She was both relieved and guiltily touched by Gordon's reaction to what he regarded as his present.

'Give me a shout when it's ready, Mary, and I'll carry the tray in,' Gordon said, pulling up the winged chair from beside the telephone and sitting himself down opposite the three men.

He was in a high humour. He caught her hand as she passed his chair and squeezed her fingers.

While she measured out the coffee and switched on the percolator Gordon's voice and Shaw's drifted in to her. She heard Gordon apologize for his informal garb, heard Shaw ask about the University, whether he was now on holiday, and then Gordon expounding on the house. The improvements they'd managed up to now, and what he intended to do.

Was it very lonely, Shaw asked. Or did the family enjoy being surrounded by woods? The coffee had begun to perk. She watched the brown liquid bubble and burst into the little glass dome. It always reminded her of blood pulsing in some distended aneurysm of a vein. She thought suddenly of the hare. And the bright blood all over the kitchen floor.

'Ready yet, dear?'

'Yes, just about.'

'Seem quite nice fellows,' he murmured, coming in and leaning on the dresser, watching her as she took some biscuits out of a tin and arranged them on the plate. 'All set? I'll take the tray if you bring the pot.'

He waved her to precede him. The three men were sitting exactly as she left them. Two on the sofa, one in the big leather armchair. As family or friends usually sat, grouped round the coffee table. Eyes fixed on the kitchen doorway.

Except that they didn't look relaxed or friendly any more. And neither family nor friends ever sat with revolvers in their hands.

'Your present, Professor Greville,' Mr Shaw said, pointing to the coloured photograph now unwrapped and propped on the mantelpiece. 'Is it not beautiful?'

Fallowlands – from five hundred feet a red-brick centre surrounded by a green frame of trees, the tall Tudor chimneys sending their shadows over the old tiles, the bright balustraded rectangle of the balcony outside Rowena's room.

But all Gordon Greville said was, 'Is this some sort of joke?'

'Joke, Mr Greville?'

'Is it?' Mary echoed. The tray with the second-best black and white coffee cups trembled in her hands. 'No . . . I can see it's not.'

'Mrs Greville . . . *please*.' Shaw went over to her as she stood beside Gordon in the doorway. 'There's nothing to be frightened about. Allow me.' He took the tray, put it on the coffee table, and began to pour out three cups. 'How kind!' While his two friends helped themselves, he lifted his own cup to his lips. 'Delicious! Now Professor and Mrs Greville, please do sit down. And I will explain.'

'If you want money . . .' Gordon reached for his wallet. Shaw shook his head. 'Not money.'

'Silver . . . we've quite a bit of Georgian . . .'

Shaw continued to shake his head, smiled reproachfully. 'Jewellery . . .'

'Mr Greville, we are not thieves!'

'Then what are you?' Mary asked sharply.

'Have you heard of outcasts, Mrs Greville?'

'Yes.'

'That is all we are.'

'Then what are you doing with those guns?'

'Nothing, Mrs Greville. I promise you, nothing. So long as . . .'

'What?'

'You and your family . . . see our point of view.'

'What are you trying to tell us?' Gordon did his best to speak slowly and calmly. After all, they might be mad. He tried to think if there had been any warnings of escapes from Broadmoor recently. None that he could think of, but there were those two convicts who'd shinned over the wall at Maidstone gaol a week ago. And a month ago, those three IRA men who'd been sprung from Wormwood Scrubs. They had never been caught.

'Professor Greville,' Shaw said. 'We know you for a humanitarian . . . a man who supports the underdog, who believes in justice.'

'There are also things I do not believe in.'

'Such as?'

'Guns.'

'Oh, is it these toys that are troubling you?' Shaw laughed and murmured something to the other two. Immediately all three of them put their revolvers away into some holster under their coats. 'Now, is that better?'

'Yes.'

Shaw drained his cup, put it back on the saucer. 'That was very nice, Mrs Greville.'

'Tell us who you are and what you want.'

'Please, Professor! Was it not agreed that we would have a nice friendly talk?'

'Are you political refugees?'

Shaw inclined his head. 'You could call us that.'

'Illegal immigrants?'

'You could call us that, too.'

'Have you escaped from prison?'

'Professor, I have escaped from many prisons.'

'I take it the police . . .'

Shaw held up his hand. 'Quite, Professor. How quickly you understand! We do not wish to meet the police. Indeed we do not wish to meet anybody.' He smiled. 'Except, of course, you and your charming family.'

'You wish to hide here?'

'Hide?' Shaw winced. 'Rather we wish to be your guests.'

'For how long?'

'Six days.'

'And then you will leave?'

'I promise.'

Gordon rummaged in the pocket of his old dressing-gown, found his empty pipe and tapped it against his teeth. 'I am beginning to understand what it is you need.'

'I was sure you would.'

'Three hundred years ago – ' he had found his tin of Golden Flake now, was stuffing the shreds of tobacco into the bowl of his pipe – 'priests were hidden here. From Cromwell's soldiery.'

'Does not history repeat itself?'

'But the householder then was also Catholic.'

'Professor Greville . . . you are a peacemaker?'

'I am a believer in one world.'

'So am I, Professor.'

'What you are asking us to do – ' Gordon lit his pipe slowly – 'is to break the laws of our own society and give you sanctuary.'

'I am not asking you to break your laws. I am simply asking your hospitality for five and a half days. Undisturbed.'

'For what reason?'

'So that we can take leave of your country.'

'Without the police finding you?'

Shaw inclined his head.

'So you *are* on the run?'

For the third time, Shaw inclined his head.

'What I want to know is – ' Gordon nodded at the photograph of Fallowlands – 'why you went to so much trouble to select *this* house? Was it because it was so isolated?'

'Professor Greville.' Shaw smiled. 'You perceive everything!'

'And if . . . and it is a big if, Mr Shaw . . . we agree that you should remain here as our . . . undisturbed guests . . . will you promise to go when you say?'

'We will leave on Monday morning . . . I promise.'

'And what will you give us in return, Mr Shaw?'

'Our friendship.'

'By that – ' Professor Greville pursed his mouth and then let out a puff of blue tobacco smoke from the left-hand side of his lips – 'I understand you to mean that no harm shall come to any of my family.'

'That is perfectly correct, Professor.'

'Well . . . now at least we understand each other.'

'Then you will also understand that we will have to take . . . certain precautions.'

'Such as?'

'No one must be allowed to come inside the house. And . . . regrettably . . . none of your family must go outside.'

'We are to be prisoners in our own home?'

Shaw wrinkled up his face in distaste. 'I do not like the word "prisoner", Professor. We are all to be one happy family. But there have to be . . . certain rules. And these rules must be obeyed. Otherwise . . .' Just for a second his hand went inside his jacket pocket. 'However you are all too sensible, I am sure.'

He smiled at Gordon. 'And now if you would ask the rest of your charming family to come down and meet their guests?'

Over the rim of his coffee cup Shaw watched Gordon Greville walk across the polished oak boards to the staircase. 'Of course,' he called after him, still smiling, 'if any of you should attempt to give the alarm, I shall kill your wife.' He took out his gun and pointed it almost playfully at Mary's head. The other two took out theirs.

'You have my word,' Gordon replied.

'A charming man,' Shaw said to Mary. 'A man of – how shall I put it – honour? Yes?'

Mary nodded, and stared at her clasped hands. 'Don't you think,' she blurted out after a moment, 'that it'll be noticed? If none of us appears in the village? If none of us ever goes out?'

Shaw glanced at her abstractedly for a while. Then his dark eyes left her face. There was the sound of slippered feet on the top of the staircase. The creak of the old boards. The family procession slowly descended. First Eleanor, looking plump and pregnant in a pink quilted dressing-gown, dopey with the tablets Dr Mason had given her. Ginny, head high, nostrils pinched, her angry eyes fixed in horror on the silent fawn-suited man. Then Rowena, her face blotchy with sleep. After them came Gordon and Richard side by side. For some reason Gordon was holding their son's arm. Yet there was no need. That was apparent. And the boy seemed to be dragging him along like some moth-eaten old teddy-bear who wouldn't be discarded.

Young Richard stood for a moment, taking in the scene below him. He looked from the guns to the gunmen's faces, from Shaw to his two silent henchmen, and then back to the guns again.

He looked at first bewildered, then surprised, then almost gratified. Then he smiled slowly, almost admiringly. And sensing an unexpected ally John Shaw crooked his finger and smiled invitingly back.


'Tell me it isn't happening,' Eleanor whispered to Ginny in the twin bed beside her.

'For safety,' so the gunman said, the females of the family had been put into the parents' room while Gordon Greville and his son slept in Richard's. The gunmen had dragged two extra beds inside, and stood over Ginny while she made them up. She could still feel their eyes on her, the different way they looked at her from the way they looked at her two sisters. They made her feel sick, her skin crawl. She dared not let herself contemplate what might happen before Monday.

'Ssh,' Ginny whispered. 'Go to sleep. Don't think about it. If we're careful, it should be all right.'

But it wouldn't be. She knew that. There was more to all this than illegal immigrant running. More than just holing up. Why otherwise had that same fawn-suited man, who now sat on guard outside on the landing, so carefully followed her? Had he followed her before? Had he followed other members of the family? Maybe for weeks? Built up a dossier of their activities? Her father would have been too vague and abstracted to notice. Her mother too busy.

And the photo of Fallowlands. Was that part of an elaborate plan? An entry to the house, an excuse for meticulous observation of every detail, its isolation from the village – its long approach from the lane, its security, or lack of it? How else could they have come supplied with the right padlocks to secure the diamond-paned double-glazed windows so suffocatingly tight? How else could they be so knowledgeable about the lay-out of the rooms, even the potential of the tiny landing window from which Rowena loved to spy on her dates?

But for what was all this to be used? What made Fallowlands so special?

'Do you really think they'll go?' Eleanor whispered.
'Yes.'
'On Monday?'
'Yes.'
'Bill would kill them if he found them still here.'
'I know. But he won't. They'll be gone.'

'If only he'd been here *now*,' Eleanor wailed softly, and then began to cry. Ginny didn't try to stop her. As a child Eleanor was always the gentle weepy one who had the knack of purging her troubles in tears and then drifting off to sleep. In a little while Ginny heard Eleanor's more gentle breathing.

'Is she asleep?' Mary sat up in bed, whispering just loud enough for Ginny to hear.

'Yes.'

'It's her I'm most worried about . . . the shock. God knows what it might do!'

'Ssh . . . don't talk about it!'

'But what will Bill think? It's *my* fault. And your father's. We should never have let them in. Why ever did I say I'd have their wretched photo?'

'They'd have found some other means,' Ginny breathed. 'They were determined to get in.'

'Because it's so isolated d'you mean?'

'Yes.'

Mary Greville sighed. 'Even so . . . Eleanor's bound to suffer. All this strain. And being shut in like this. At her particular time.' She turned towards the padlocked windows. A handful of stars glittered between the undrawn curtains. How many million light years away? Beyond the woodland would be a few village lights, and they too might have been as distant.

'She should be over the worst.'

'But I had a miss at four months. After Rowena.'

'I know. Still, you got Richard in the end.'

Mary sighed again heavily. Yes, she'd got Richard. And a strange blessing or curse he had proved to be. The son of the house. Born to supplant the father. Strike the father dead. Why did she think that? She shivered in the stiflingly hot room, remembering the crushed and bloody head of the dying hare. Remembering that odd look on Richard's face when he came downstairs to meet the gunmen just four hours ago.

What had that look been? Astonished surprise? Delight? Empathy? As if all his secret adolescent life, he had dreamed and longed for something like this to happen.

It was all too much to bear. Mary Greville quailed inside herself, aching to abdicate her role of matron and mother. To cry and go to Ginny of all people to be comforted.

She punched her pillow fretfully. It was almost dawn. She could hear the first tentative pipe of bird song.

'Take one of Eleanor's sleeping pills,' Ginny suggested. 'They're here on the dressing-table.'

'Will you have one, too?'

'Yes.' Ginny uncapped the bottle and shook out a couple of pills. She took one over to her mother, a pale slender figure in a short white frilled nightgown.

Mary Greville had not missed the looks the gunmen had fastened on her daughter. But she somehow dared not acknowledge them to herself. Dared not contemplate to what their interest might lead. Dared not? Would not.

'That's a useless sort of nightgown,' she said, sharply.

'*I* like it. And it's cool. Here, have a sip of Eleanor's water to get that pill down. How about Rowena?'

'She's out like a light.'

'Lucky her!' Ginny climbed back into bed. 'What it is to be young and foolish,' she added with an attempt at her old manner. Then she lay back on her pillow, staring up at the ceiling, and waited for the gentle fuzz of the sedative to blur out the memory of the gunmen's eyes, and her own terrifying picture of the immediate future.


Rowena was not in fact asleep. She lay nearest the door and facing it, with her head shrouded in the top sheet. Her eyes were fixed on the crack of light visible under the old oak door.

For the first hour a shadow had travelled every few minutes along it and back again, like a blob of expanding and contracting mercury. There was the soft creak of stockinged feet. Rowena slid her hand from under the covers and looked at the luminous dial of her wrist-watch. Four-fifteen. A mile away cowmen would be driving cattle into the milking parlours, the postmen would be collecting the mail. An early jet flight was homing in on Grantwick, and in the woods and the hedges and the garden the dawn chorus had splendidly begun.

Sparrow chirps and blackbird and robin song joining the first warblings of the hedge birds. Inside the room her mother and sisters drifted off. Eleanor was snuffling and crying out in her dreams, but staying asleep.

Then she heard a sound that she thought at first was another aircraft approaching. A broken-off sound. A very reassuring human sound. Rowena smiled to herself in the darkness. The guard on the landing was asleep at last.

Cautiously Rowena pushed back the covers and swung her legs out of bed. Already the stars had vanished. The sky paled. Not dawn yet. But first light. The time for deeds and high adventure. Quietly she reached the door.

Before going to bed, she had already greased the hinges and the handle with dollops of Ginny's extra thick face cream. Rowena turned the handle now, slowly and skilfully, without sound.

The door opened inwards. Bit by bit, she eased it back. The fawn-suited man was asleep in the velvet-covered tub chair from Ginny's room. He still wore his glasses, but he'd taken off his hat. His hair was black and smooth and shiny like a black cap. One hand was flung wide. She could see the holster held with snap studs to the inside of his jacket, and the sweat staining the armpit of his shirt. His thin mouth was open, and his head moved as he snored as if any moment he might frighten himself awake.

Horrible! Not that he frightened her. Disgusted her more likely. A thin sly runt of a man. Not the man that had been living in the woods. One of them was, she felt sure. But not him. Over the days she had come to feel she knew that man. Occasionally she'd left him food. Held imaginary conversations with him. Sat in that same wood and told him in his invisible absence about the bloody awful Biology paper, her certain failure, about Richard's total bloodiness, about herself and her frustrations. She held that man in some sort of relationship. Almost romantic.

Cautiously, with her eyes on the man's face, her body in its sensible cotton nightdress pressed against the landing wall. That was where the floor joists were strongest and the boards creaked less. She eased herself past him. She could actually see her own white reflection move across his spectacles, and for a split second she froze in terror, interpreting it as the movement of eyeballs. She was so close that if she stretched out her hand she could have just touched the butt of his revolver. But even if she'd reached it, she wouldn't have known what to do.

At the top of the stairs, she paused and looked down. All lights were out, the ground floor deserted. The front door was illuminated by the wide shaft of light from the landing, and visible from where the gunman sat. The telephone on the other hand was not. It was tucked inside the sitting-room, on the low table with the photos. When the sitting-room wall was partly demolished to open the room up into the hall, they had left a small corner either side. One for Mary's desk, the other a cosy private place for the telephone.

Rowena gave one last look at the snoring gunman, drew one last deep breath to calm her heartbeat, and trod the first stair.

Descending was like an old-fashioned ballroom dance. One down and two paces to the left. A long stride to miss the

59

next step with the weak tread. Three more in quick succession, dead centre. Four more to the left, one treading on the right. Rowena knew every creak and fault on that staircase. Rather as she knew every creak and fault of her ghastly family. She'd never dwelt on her own. She acknowledged that she must have them. But so far they hadn't made themselves clear to her.

At the bottom, she gave a quick glance over her shoulder. Everything remained still. The snores came louder and more established. The house proclaimed sleep. Rowena crossed the hall with only slightly less care, weaving around the known danger spots. But she was still shaking from her careful descent of the stairs. Her mouth was dry, too, though she refused to believe she was afraid. She went under the big beam that separated the sitting-room, and out of the borrowed landing light.

It was very dark and she had not anticipated that they would alter the furniture around. She had a mental map, and the map was changed. She stubbed her bare toes against the leg of a chair, and froze in terror. Nothing moved. No one called out. The snoring continued faintly from the landing. She stood with her arms clasped around herself, letting her eyes get used to the darkness, picking out the more solid black of furniture. Then slowly she picked her new course to the corner and the telephone.

That hadn't been changed. Her fingers found the instrument. She waited, screwing up her courage, pulled her padded dressing gown round it like a tea-cosy to muffle the slight ring and the ratcheting sound.

She knew exactly what she was going to do. She was going to dial 999, and when they asked her whether she wanted the police, fire brigade or the ambulance, she was going to say 'All three.'

She lifted the receiver.

At least she almost lifted it. A hand fastened over her wrist with considerable force, and wrenched her hand round. She gave a quickly stifled gasp of pain. Her other wrist was seized, clasped together in the man's hand. She heard the clink of the table lamp, blinked her eyes in the flood of light. She saw John Shaw, still dressed, kick back the wing chair he'd obviously been sitting in by the telephone. His hair was rumpled as if he might have been trying to rest. Then, before she'd time to think any more, two things happened simultaneously. The guard on the landing woke, and Shaw hit her hard across the jaw with the wrist of his right hand. Her teeth snapped together trapping her tongue, her head jerked, blood came into her mouth. But she managed not to scream.

She heard the guard on the landing creaking noisily down the stairs, calling some interrogative. What if the whole house awoke? What would the gunmen do? Why, come to that, hadn't her father wakened? Why was it all so quiet? Was everybody dead? Terror began to seep up through her like cold water rising.

Shaw watched her face carefully. Without taking his eyes from hers he called something unintelligible over to the gunman with the dark glasses. Slowly and reluctantly, the feet creaked back upstairs.

'What did you say to him?' Rowena whispered.

'That is my business.'

'Please tell me.'

'Very well.' His grip on her wrists tightened painfully. He laid the cold barrel of his gun against her cheek. 'I said I could deal with you myself. That is so, is it not?'

'I suppose so.'

'What they call summary justice.'

'Are you going to kill me?' Rowena's mouth felt dry as bran, but she could feel a little trickle of blood in the corners.

'That might be a waste,' Shaw brought out his handkerchief and wiped her lips. 'That better?'

She nodded.

'After all, I said justice. We do not yet know the crime.'

Rowena shrugged.

'Was it that you were going to phone? Break your word? Give the alarm. Betray us?'

Rowena shrugged.

Shaw stroked her cheek with the gun. 'Answer!'

'Yes.'

'Guilty then?'

'Yes.'

'So I must sentence you.'

'Only me,' Rowena said. 'You won't do anything to the others?'

'No. Only you. They stay safe. They behave. But I must sentence you. Otherwise my colleagues – ' He sighed heavily. 'But we have mitigating circumstances. First, you are young. Immature. Second – ' he smiled. 'You have been so far helpful. You have won the judge's friendship.'

'How?'

'Obedience. Assistance to a stranger in the woods.'

She looked up at him, her eyes wide. 'It was you, was it?'

'Of course. The judge formed a good impression of you. He is only disappointed that you did not live up to it.'

'I'm sorry.'

'That is two of us then.'

'Yes.'

'You would not want to see your friend in the woods shut up like a tame rabbit.'

'No, of course not.'

'Then you will never again betray me?'

'Never!'

'In that case your sentence is this.'

Abruptly Shaw released her wrists, seized her by the shoulders and kissed her on her mouth. His tongue tried to force in between her lips. His body pressed on hers. It was a kiss to degrade and humiliate.

She felt sick, cheapened, outraged. But it was he in the end who pushed her away.

'There!' he said, laughing. 'I think we shall teach you to grow more mature and older by Monday. I think you will learn something from us, my little false friend.'


A rapid succession of small sounds brought Gordon Greville back to full wakefulness – a quick exchange in what sounded like some Slavonic language, the creak of feet on the stairs, the scraping of a chair. A distant murmur that might have been voices but it was difficult to say with the thickness of the walls.

Gordon lay back for a while on his pillow in the second bed. Early morning light was filtering through the hessian weft of the drawn curtains in Richard's room, bringing up out of the darkness the German helmet over the fireplace, the scale models of tanks and weaponry that crowded the window-sill, the general unspeakable mess that covered the floor and his so-called work table, the flamboyant coloured photograph of Che Guevara on the far wall. Six hours earlier, bathed then in electric light, such a sight had no doubt gladdened the heart of Shaw and his henchmen, though as always, it depressed Gordon. But all he said was, 'I think they'll play the game.'

There was no reply from Richard, though he knew he was awake.

'That is, if we play the game too.'

'What game, Father? Cricket?'

If only Richard had indeed devoted his energy to such natural outlets for aggression, this room might not now resemble a psychotic nightmare. But live and let live was Gordon's motto. Children must develop naturally. And he had always made it clear that his son could do what he liked with his room, so long as no guns or offensive weapons were brought into the house.

'You know quite well what I mean, Richard.'

'No, I don't think I do, Father.'

Gordon sighed, lifted his head from the pillow and clasped his hands behind it. Sometimes he wondered if Richard and he spoke the same language. 'What I am trying to say is that at least they don't appear to be maniacs.'

'Why should they be?'

'That was my first thought. But the man Shaw is educated.'

'Eton or Harrow, Father?'

'This is hardly the time for being funny.'

'I wasn't trying to be.'

'Nor were you succeeding.'

'Well, then?'

'All that I meant to convey was that he appeared susceptible to reason.'

'That is *your* definition of educated, Father?'

Gordon sighed. 'We won't go into all that now. I am simply trying to say that he is the kind of man with whom we can communicate. Come to terms with.'

'Especially when he's got a Smith and Wesson 7.65mm in his hand. Super weapon, that. High velocity. Tiny perforation. Minimal bleeding.'

Gordon closed his eyes. He might have been listening to his own father grown mysteriously young. With grinding patience he went on, 'But I'm not sure about the other two.'

'They're not British, Father, would you say?'

'No.' Gordon ignored his son's tone. 'The big chap could be anything. The sallow one with the glasses looks Italian.'

'They've got Lugers. Did you notice that? Magazines in the stock. Deadly!'

'I'm not interested frankly in their guns. I'm interested in *them*. What they're up to.'

Richard gave a sharp, unamused laugh. 'What *are* they up to?'

'They're on the run.'

'What from? A murder?'

Gordon shook his head. 'They don't look the sort. More likely bringing illegal immigrants. Or they themselves are illegal immigrants.'

'Then they *are* maniacs, Father. Mad as bloody hatters. Who would want to be British today?'

Gordon drew in a long noisy breath. 'You young people don't know how well off you are.'

'In this filthy rotten society, Father?'

'In this green and pleasant and civilized land, Richard.'

'Green with mould, Father.' Richard threw back his bed-clothes. 'And what about the rest of the bloody world? The Indians? That sallow chap looks to me like a Pakistani! And what about the West Bank refugees?'

'We give what we can.'

'Money, bloody money! That's no good.'

'The Arabs anyway, Richard, have enough money to transform the Jordan into –'

'What, Father? The Hanging Gardens of Babylon?'

'If you like.'

'But it won't be flowers hanging there, Father.'

'I know, I know, Richard . . . it'll be the villains of the Western World. Your mother and me included.'

Richard got out of bed, stood up and stretched. 'One day the youth of the world –'

'Will unite. Yes, Richard. You've told us. Many times. I only wish they'd hurry up and get on with it.'

'Maybe sooner than you think.' Richard padded over to the washbasin and urinated.

'Orders.' He spoke to his father's scandalized reflection in the mirror above the basin. 'We're not to go on to the landing without permission. Remember? I'm playing the game. Father. I'm peeing where I'm told to. Isn't that what it's all about?'

Impressively patient, Gordon drew back the curtains. The morning, weatherwise at least, promised fair. A dark egg-yolk sun was rising through the south-east spinney of young poplar trees. There was a faint hazing of mist – heat mist by the look of it. Mary's hollyhocks and delphiniums had not been beaten by last night's rain, he was glad to see. The thick tongues of the rhododendron leaves glistened almost white behind the bed of brilliant orange geraniums. Mary was so right. There was immense solace in a garden. The birds sang, bees and butterflies flitted around the many-coloured flowers about their normal business. He watched a squirrel run up the big oak, along the branch, and then jump joyfully from the oak to a beech. Then from the beech to a willow to a walnut tree.

Gordon felt enormously refreshed, calmed in spirit. The Gospel of nature. 'Lovely morning,' he said peaceably as his son came up and stood beside him.

Just below and to the left the garage door banged shut. Gordon Greville saw the big red-haired fellow coming across the concrete from the garage. He stopped just below the window and looked around him. Raised his hand as if to shade his eyes. Moved no doubt, as Gordon Greville was, by the beauty of the morning. Noticing the colours of the garden. Watching, like another human being, the movement of the invisible squirrel among the thick leaves of the willow, its emergence along a half-dead branch. Its leap to the beech, its leap . . . no, it's *half* leap to the oak.

In mid-air the squirrel faltered, tossed itself up, paws wide, spreadeagled against the sun.

Then down it plummeted into the leafy undergrowth.

The red-haired man smiled, slipped the revolver back under his jacket.

'What a shot!' Richard exclaimed. 'Hellishly difficult, I can tell you.'

'But I didn't hear anything,' Gordon complained as if to the referee of some game. 'Just a slight thud.'

'Silencer.' Richard shook his head in admiration. 'They don't miss a trick, do they?'

He rasped his fingers over his face, stared at himself in the mirror as if he had nothing more important on his mind than wondering if he should bother to shave.


'Normalcy,' Shaw said.

Outside, blue sky, not a breath of wind. Rooks were circling noisily high above the elms.

'Normalcy.' Shaw smiled and listened, as though he was conducting an orchestra on an old familiar tune. But it was not a baton that he waved in his hand but a 7.65mm Luger. 'Everyone understand?'

His dark eyes scrutinized the faces around him in the cruel mid-morning light. Mary and Eleanor, pale and stunned. Gordon sitting on the sofa with his arms folded, nodding his head as though to make clear that he understood. Rowena had tilted her head to one side, looking at Shaw through half-closed lids. Richard sat quite still, inscrutable as ever. Only Ginny glared defiantly back at him, her head held high.

'Normalcy . . . you will go about your business with normalcy. We will go about ours. Then we shall all be one big happy family . . . and no one will get hurt.'

They had had a quick breakfast of coffee and toast and marmalade. Since all knives and anything that could be used as a weapon had been removed, Mrs Greville had taken an already sliced packet of bread from the deep freeze. The meal had been eaten all together round the kitchen table in complete silence. Ginny and Rowena had washed up. Mrs

Greville and Eleanor had made the beds. The big red-haired gunman and the one in the dark glasses had gone into the garage and closed the door.

'We want your cooperation. Understand, Professor Greville?'

'Understood, but . . .'

'Professor Greville, you are known for your liberal views. A tolerant man. Not a Christian but a Humanist. These things, we believe too.'

'I am glad to hear it.'

'You are one of us, Professor.'

'No, no.' Gordon produced his pipe, perhaps as a symbol of peace, to wave side by side with Shaw's gun. 'You musn't get me wrong. I don't approve of what you're doing. Far from it! But I think I understand your motives.'

'What you are saying is you will do business with us?'

'It is Hobson's Choice.'

'Who is this Hobson?'

'It is simply a saying meaning that I have no option.'

'You are wise enough to see that none of your family must resist?'

Gordon raised his pipe. 'Provided – '

'Provided?'

'You know what I mean. In any bargain there is a *quid pro quo*.'

'Of course. Of course. If you and your family do as you are told and continue with normalcy, I have said no harm will come to any of you.'

'This you promise?'

'This I promise.'

'How can I believe you?'

'You have to believe me, Professor Greville. But I say this . . . the moment you see I am lying . . . kill me, kill us all.'

'With what?' Ginny asked.

'You will keep this girl quiet, Professor Greville!' Shaw said sharply. 'I shall see that my men behave. You shall see that your family behave. Last night, Rowena – ' His eyes as they turned on her softened and almost twinkled. 'Oh yes, the naughty girl, I caught her trying to telephone! Well, we can be understanding, too, and you see nothing happened to her. But no more! You will all do as you are told. No raising an alarm. No trying to escape.'

There was a silence. Outside in the garden starlings quarrelled noisily. Overhead came the whistle of turbo-props as the eleven o'clock Fokker Friendship from Amsterdam descended down the glide path.

'You understand, Professor Greville?'

Inside the house there was still silence.

'If you do *not* understand, then we have no option. Normalcy, that is what I have asked for. We do not want to see you all trussed like chickens, but we have rope if necessary. We have *other* things.' He paused. 'But all these we want to forget. We want to be friends. We want you to move round the house quite freely. We don't want to interfere with you, if you don't interfere with us. Your business, our business. What could be fairer, Professor Greville?'

Gordon tapped his pipe out in his hand. 'Point taken.'

'But we don't know what his business is!' Ginny said.

The gunman walked across and furiously waved the Luger at her. 'That is what I fear! Such an attitude! Our business is *our* business! We have told you all we can . . . and there is still this distrust. In that case, Professor Greville – '

Shaw took hold of Ginny's right arm and twisted it behind her back.

'Now, now, now,' Gordon said. 'Don't let's get all excited! This is a situation. An unwelcome one from our point of view, but one to which we must accommodate. We have your word that no harm will come to us. In return, we will do what you say and not interfere.'

'*All* of you.'

'All of us.' Gordon Greville looked round his family and said gently, 'We must do this. We cannot do otherwise. We must obey. It is a sort of parole he is asking us for. If one of us breaks parole, the others will suffer, perhaps grievously.' He turned to Shaw. 'We will obey you.'

The gunman released Ginny's arm. The smile returned to his face. 'There!' he said. 'I knew you would understand. You are a gentleman, my brother. We will shake hands on this, yes?'

'All right.'

Shaw laid down his gun. Gordon laid down his pipe. Across the table, they shook hands.

'Now,' Shaw said, 'we can make our plans. You, Professor, had you any arrangements today?'

'None.'

'You.' He pointed to Eleanor. 'No clinics? No doctors?'

The voice was almost inaudible. 'No.'

'I,' Ginny said, 'should go to Art College.'

'That is all right. It is taken care of. A message has been left.' He turned to Mary. 'And you, Mrs Greville? What were you doing today?'

'Just things in the house.'

'Anyone coming to tea . . . to drinks?'

'No.'

'Anyone coming during the next four days?'

'No one has been invited. But I do the church flowers on Friday. It would be noticed . . .'

'You – ' Shaw turned away from Mary to give Rowena a dazzling smile ' – are home for the holidays. Southly High School . . . oh yes, we too have done our homework! But you – ' He turned to Richard. 'Term at Westley Grammar does not end till Friday.'

Richard shrugged. 'Often have a couple of days off without

70

even asking.'

'All the same,' Shaw addressed Mary. 'Telephone. Tell them he's unwell. You want to see that he is better for going away on your holiday.'

'*What* holiday?'

'We will come to that presently. Now telephone the school.' He waved her over to the corner of the kitchen, watching her trembling hands open the telephone book and hold it close to her eyes.

'Have you got your glasses, my dear?' her husband said. 'Here, borrow mine!'

'Stay where you are! You!' He pointed to Ginny. 'Go and help your mother.'

Ginny jumped up. Deliberately, she had put on a pair of old corduroy trousers and a loose-fitting artist's smock, but she could feel his eyes take in every movement she made as she crossed the floor and bent over her mother.

'There . . . 2375!'

'What's the code?'

'Nine.'

When her mother lifted the telephone, Shaw ordered Ginny back to her chair with a jerk of his head.

He listened carefully as Mary Greville asked for the Head-master's secretary.

'And be convincing,' he whispered. 'Don't try anything.'

'Oh,' Mary Greville replied in a high frightened voice to something said by the Headmaster's secretary. 'Did I sound worried? No, I'm not at all really. It's just a tummy upset. But we're going on holiday and . . .'

When she put down the receiver, she leaned for a moment with her elbows on the table and her head in her hands. The table shook with her trembling.

'I'm not much good at this sort of thing!' She spread her hands on the table and sent Shaw a look of wild, desperate apology.

'Then you will just have to learn. Now next this number . . . Ramsgate 4532. It is a boat hire firm. They know you will telephone. You are confirming the hire of a thirty-foot cabin cruiser for your fortnight's holiday, starting next Monday. You will arrive on the quay at noon.'

Mary was so nervous that she dialled a wrong number. Immediately Shaw was suspicious. Next time she got it right, passed on the message to a bored-sounding girl who told her that the boat was called *Kittiwake* and would be fitted up ready to leave.

When she replaced the receiver Shaw said kindly, 'You were better that time. Before you go, you will do it with great . . .' He gestured with his hands, searching for the right word.

'Aplomb,' said Rowena.

'Thank you.' Shaw drew in a deep breath. 'Now we are all taken care of . . .' He paused while a jet whined low in the circuit.

'The church flowers?' Mary asked nervously. 'I really must . . .'

'Can you not make an excuse?'

'They'd think it odd.'

'Very well. I will *consider* it. Meanwhile let me tell you how we will continue. We shall have a programme . . . one that is convenient to *you*.' He pointed to them and then to himself. 'And to us. When do you have your meals, Mrs Greville?'

'Breakfast at seven forty-five. Lunch at one. Supper at eight.'

'That will be admirable. We will all eat in the dining-room. The women will prepare the meals and serve them. Have you enough food, Mrs Greville?'

'There's enough in the deep freeze. But I was keeping it low to put in produce. There's plenty of vegetables in the garden, tomatoes in the greenhouse.'

'My men will pick vegetables.'

'Why not us?' Mary asked. 'We must have exercise.'

'And you shall, Mrs Greville. The best exercise in the world.'

'And what is that?'

'Digging.'

'But Eleanor, she must have rest.'

'And so she shall, Mrs Greville. That too shall be organized. And now, the milkman?'

'Tomorrow and Friday.'

'What about newspapers?'

'We are too far away. There is no delivery.'

'So that is all?'

'Except the postman.'

'When?'

'Every morning. But he doesn't come to the house. He leaves the letters in the box at the far end of the drive.'

'That's all right then. But for the milkman you will leave a note tomorrow to say that you are going off on holiday and want no more milk for fourteen days. I will dictate the note, you understand?'

'Yes.'

'Now during the day, you will all stay in the house. The women will do the domestic work as usual. But otherwise, you may do as you like. Professor Greville . . . no doubt you will wish to stay in your study. Your daughter – ' he was looking at Ginny ' – no doubt will be inspired to paint. Rowena – ' he smiled as he said it – 'will wish to continue her studies in the lounge.'

'Why not my room?'

'We need your room.'

'But my desk's there ! And all my books !'

'You may remove what you want.'

'But why *my* room?'

Shaw did not answer.

'What are you going to *do* in Rowena's room?' Ginny asked.

'That is none of your business,' Shaw said abruptly.

'It isn't fair!' said Rowena. 'Why don't you take Richard's room?'

'It is not your room. It is *our* room. Where we sleep. Out of bounds to you all. No one must come beyond the staircase on the landing.'

'What about the balcony?' Ginny persisted.

'That, too, is out of bounds.'

'Going to sunbathe?' asked Rowena.

A brilliant white-toothed smile. 'But of course!'

'What about me?' said Richard. 'What can I do?'

'You have not been forgotten.' Shaw said. 'You can stay with us and – '

'As a hostage?' Mary interrupted.

'Of course not, Mrs Greville! As a comrade. He is strong, we will need his help. Moving things. We will need the help of all of you. Perhaps some time my colleagues and I wish to disappear. The police . . . you understand. One cannot be too careful. Your cellar . . . so useful. So . . .'

'Inconspicuous,' said Rowena.

'Thank you.' Shaw inclined his head. 'You will all perhaps help to make it comfortable. A chair or two. Beds. A table. Nothing elaborate. Just . . . just – '

'Just in case,' said Rowena.

Again Shaw gave a polite little nod in her direction. 'If you wouldn't mind?'

'Of course not,' Gordon Greville said.

'Thank you . . . thank you. I appreciate this co-operation. Now there is only one more thing. You have a home help, I believe, Mrs Greville?'

Mary nodded, 'Mrs Bristowe.'

'But only once a week?'

'Yes.'

'When does she come?'

'Tomorrow.'

'Where does she live?'

'The other side of the village. The watermill cottage. Three miles away.'

'Telephone her.'

'She is not on the phone.'

'Telephone her neighbours.'

'She has no near neighbours.'

'Then you must write a letter. Now . . . immediately!'

'I have no paper.'

'In my study,' Gordon said. 'Rowena – '

'Permission.' She turned her head. 'Please, sir?'

Shaw smiled and nodded. She was back in a moment. 'Paper . . . stamps . . . envelope.'

'There, Mrs Greville.' Shaw said as she picked up the pen. 'I am reading every word. Good . . . good! That is sufficient. Now the address.'

He examined the paper carefully, held it to the light before putting it in the envelope.

'Where is the posting box?'

'Down the lane,' Mary said. 'Five minutes' walk.'

'I'll take it,' said Rowena.

'No . . . the boy.' Shaw handed the letter to Richard, who stood up with alacrity. 'I can trust you?'

'Sure.'

'You won't try anything?'

'Nothing.'

'All the same . . .' Through the frosted glass window of the door to the outer kitchen could be seen the muzzy shadow of the fawn-suited man. 'You will go with our colleague.'

Richard shrugged. 'All the same to me.'

'Be quick.'

'I will be.' Almost eagerly, Richard started for the door. For the first time in his life, Gordon Greville thought, watching his son wryly, Richard is doing immediately exactly what he's told.

'I am shocked, Mrs Greville.'

'Why, Mr Shaw?'

'At you and the Professor keeping sodium chlorate in the garage.'

'It is simply a weed killer.'

'It is also highly poisonous. Also explosive. It has been removed.' Shaw came across to her as she stood in front of the corner of boiled gammon, the lettuce, tomatoes, radishes and cucumber, trying to work out how to make a ham salad without knives or forks. 'Is this for lunch?'

'Yes.'

He bent down and inspected the food carefully. 'That is all right. Now I wish to look at your larder.'

She led the way, opened the door. Shaw picked up a large tin on the window-sill.

'What is this?'

'Apricot puree. I picked it out for sweet. I'm sorry, but there is no cream. The milkman doesn't call till tomorrow.'

'So you have told me. I understand.' Minutely Shaw inspected every tin and jar on the shelves, looking at the labels, sniffing contents, sometimes actually tasting.

He lifted a white tin lid. 'This is bread?'

She nodded.

'Cakes, biscuits, yes, clearly labelled, I see.' He opened each tin.

'This is for fruits?'

'And fresh vegetables. Not much left, I'm afraid. But plenty in the garden.'

'What are these?'

'Mushrooms.'

'Destroy them.'

76

'They're all right. Only a bit old and – '

'*Destroy them!*' He pushed the brown paper bag into her hand. 'There . . . waste-bin.'

He watched her go across the kitchen and throw the bag into the bin.

'This is your only refrigerator?'

She nodded. He opened the door, inspected everything inside.

'Where is your deep freeze?'

'In the back kitchen.' She led the way, lifted the lid. 'Only lamb and pork and bacon left. Five loaves of bread. Three chickens. No vegetables blanched yet. We're low on everything.'

'I told you . . . we will pick more from the garden.' Again he inspected the contents microscopically. 'There is enough for us.' He straightened, told her to close the lid, led the way back into the kitchen. As he did so, he indicated the door to the boiler house, now padlocked. 'You have oil for central heating and water? No gas?'

'Only electricity.'

He held out his hands. 'Your matches.'

She took the packet from the open cupboard.

'This is all?'

'Yes.'

He pointed. 'What are those?'

'Jeyes Fluid.' She took the bottles from the shelf and held them up. 'Bleach, lysol. And this tin is metal polish.'

'Give them to me. Now upstairs.'

On the landing the sallow-faced man was keeping watch from the window that looked out on the drive – clearly on guard. Shaw said something to him, and he shook his head.

'Now first, the main bathroom!' In they went. Shaw was fascinated by the array of lipsticks, powder, scent and shampoo. He squirted the deodorants one after the other into the air.

'Very nice!' He unstoppered bottles and inhaled. A jar without its label belonging to Rowena he sniffed suspiciously, wrinkled his nose, emptied the contents down the washbasin. Then he opened the medicine chest.

Her whole armoury against calamity pathetically exposed. Bandages, boracic ointment, iodine, Algipan, Vaseline, Agarol, Vick, antiseptic cream, Coldrex, sun tan oil, Elastoplast.

'These are sleeping pills?'

'Yes. Mogadons.'

He took them.

'They are for Eleanor. And those two bottles are her vitamins.'

He took both.

'But she needs them!'

'I will dose her when necessary. And now the bathroom *en suite* with your room.'

From there he removed a packet of aspirin and a bottle of liniment, two razors and a packet of blades.

'Aren't my husband and Richard allowed to shave?'

'Razors will be allowed them each morning and returned personally to me.' Shaw turned round. 'This is everything, Mrs Greville? You do not have a store of these things?'

'No.'

'If we find anything more – ' He shook his head in mock sadness.

'There is nothing.'

'Now the bedrooms, if you please, Mrs Greville.'

Every drawer, every cupboard opened. Blouses, stockings, underclothes removed and inspected. Pockets searched. Anything remotely representing a weapon – hairpins, needles, kirbigrips, safety-pins – taken away. Brooches were removed from jewellery cases. Even the dirty washing basket was searched.

'Now, Mrs Greville, you see the sort of things I am interested in. Are there any more such things anywhere in the house?'

'No.'

'Or on your persons?'

'No.'

'Think carefully, Mrs Greville! What about your daughters?'

Mary shook her head.

'Mrs Greville, while you were in the kitchen, we searched your husband and son. We found a very nasty knife, two razor blades and five nails.'

'Richard's pockets –'

'Your son, yes. But I think you had also better ask your daughters if they are wearing any hairpins, jewellery, knives . . . oh yes, girls do these days! You understand me?'

Mary nodded.

'It is good that you do. For if we find anything on any of them, we will have you into the bathroom, one by one, and stripped.' He paused. 'I am sure you do not want that, Mrs Greville.'

She stood silent, looking at him.

'And nor do we.'

They went downstairs. Back in the kitchen, Shaw said, 'I am very glad we understand each other, Mrs Greville. You are a very sensible woman.'


'What do you really mean to do with us?' Rowena asked the fawn-suited gunman, but he looked at her blankly, shrugged his shoulders, and went on climbing the stairs. 'And why have you brought all this clobber in? And why the hell d'you have to stuff it all in *my* room?'

It was twenty-five past twelve. Only half an hour to go, thank God, before lunch. But Shaw and the fawn-suited creep were still busy sorting through the curious hessian-covered clobber they'd unloaded in the hall. Preparing, by the look of it, for one hell of a long stay. The red-haired yob had taken a not unwilling Richard outside to pull some other stuff from the Land-Rover into the garage. *Quelle* bloody mix-up.

'He won't answer you.' Shaw pushed a heavy white wooden box with his foot towards the staircase, then rested his arm on the lintel and stood smiling down at Rowena. 'So you might as well save your breath.'

'Why? Are my breaths numbered?'

'Not that I know of. Not unless you are suffering from some incurable and fatal illness.'

'Claustrophobia. I hate being confined.'

'That is not an illness. It is a state of mind.'

'I'm also dying of curiosity.'

'That *is* an illness.' Shaw smiled thinly.

'Fatal?' Rowena widened her blue eyes provocatively.

'Very. And with great rapidity. On the other hand it can be cured.' He looked away from her to say something in a low voice to the fawn-suited man who was coming down the stairs. He pointed to the box, and struggling with the weight, the man lifted it and returned upstairs.

'Mind you don't scrape my paint with it,' Rowena called after him. He didn't turn.

'Doesn't he speak English?' she asked Shaw.

'Only if he chooses.'

'What nationality is he?'

'That is of no importance.'

'Well, what's his name? He's got to have a name. Everyone's got one.'

'Hamid.'

'Pakistani?'

'Perhaps.'

'Does he have strange eating habits? You know what I mean. He isn't strictly vegetarian or Kosher, is he? Or forbidden sacred cow? Or pork? Or anything Richard's shadow's fallen on?'

Shaw laughed. 'No.'

'And what about your big red-haired chum?' She jerked her head towards the garage. 'The chappie out there with Richard?'

'He is French.'

'Like hell! *Sacré bleu!* I've tried my French on him. It didn't work.'

'Maybe you do not speak it sufficiently well.'

Rowena pulled a face.

'What's *his* name then? Rufus?'

'Kuchi.'

'Christ!'

Rowena pondered for a moment.

'Kuchi's father,' Shaw said, indicating to Hamid that he should now pick up a long thin package stitched up in hessian, 'was Albanian.'

Rowena whistled. 'Poor old Kuchi's mother! Is it true that murder and theft aren't crimes in Albania?'

'I have never asked him.' Shaw waved her to stand aside so that Hamid could manage the long parcel without knocking into her.

'And what's that?' she asked. 'It looks like a photographer's tripod. Don't tell me your trade is obscene pictures?' She put out her hand as if to touch it, till Shaw took a threatening pace forward.

'No more questions! You grow tedious and tiresome! Go help your mother with her chores!'

Scarlet-faced but with more grace than if her father had so directed her, Rowena flounced into the kitchen.


'I'm supposed to help you.'

Mary passed over to Rowena the cucumber she was trying

to cut with a spoon. 'I do wish you wouldn't talk to those men. I heard you, Rowena. You were flirting with Shaw. You mustn't. We don't really know what they're up to.'

'That's precisely what I was trying to find out.'

'You won't find out by asking. Besides we don't really know their attitudes either.'

'Such as?'

'Towards us. Towards women.'

'You mean they may not be monogamous?'

'Well, we can't afford to get familiar.'

'I've got to talk to someone. Otherwise I'll go round the twist.'

'Put on the radio.'

Half-heartedly Rowena turned the knob on the white kitchen radio. There was the hearty smack of tennis balls. 'Love forty. Oh, marvellous back-hander! Jean Latimer is really on form today.'

'Can't bear it.' Rowena switched off. 'Everyone else sounds so normal.'

Mary rolled out a cushion of pastry but said nothing. After a moment, she asked. 'Where's your father? Ginny? Eleanor? Richard?' Mary named them like someone calling the role after a shipwreck. Every ten minutes or so, isolated here in the kitchen, it swept over her like a wave of pure madness that maybe the rest of them had been quietly killed.

'Richard's with Kuchi.'

'Who?'

'The red-haired yob.'

'You're on first-name terms, are you?'

'Got to call them something, Mother.'

'And what is he doing? Richard?'

'Unloading something into the garage.'

'They're just keeping him close beside them,' Mary said softly. 'He's a hostage. In case any of us puts a foot wrong, they have him right there.' Her fingers tightened over the rolling pin. Then abruptly she pushed it to one side. She remembered what seemed like years ago and yet was only yesterday. Richard hitting the hare with that same rolling pin. The brains and the blood and the hare screaming. Obviously *they* were the sort of men Richard liked. They spoke to his condition. Nothing seemed past the young these days. Maybe Richard was like that American heiress some terrorists had captured. Staying with them. Compliant. Changed mysteriously into the likeness of her captors.

Rowena didn't contradict her. She simply went on. 'Eleanor's resting upstairs. Ginny's just gone to wash her hair. Father's being allowed to rewrite his Liberal revival lecture in the study.'

'Prisoners' privileges,' Mary muttered.

'Maybe they've been in prison themselves?'

'Ex-convicts?' Mary spooned apricot puree into the roughly fashioned plate tart and slipped it into the oven. 'Very likely.'

She switched off the hot plate under the eggs, and replaced the timer. Her hands performed everything automatically, while her feelings filled with hope and drained into despair like sand in the timer. Hope was every second bringing them nearer the end of the five days to freedom. Hope was the apparent reasonableness of Shaw. His friendliness even. Hope was his promise, so long as they kept things normal. But normal became the dreaded normalcy. And normalcy was despair. Despair was the implicit menace beneath the smiles. The guns were ready. Despair was in too careful thinking. In the question what would happen when the family was no more use? Would they kill Gordon and her? Do unspeakable things to the girls? She never dared to watch when Shaw looked at Ginny. He wanted Ginny. My God, he wanted her! And Rowena. Silly, clever Rowena! Who knew everything and knew nothing. What would they do to her? With Richard compliant, what would they do?

'You emptied your pockets?' She asked Rowena sharply, handing her the pan of eggs to cool in the sink.

'For the *fourth* time, Mother, *yes*.' Rowena tipped the eggs into the bowl, and ran cold water over them. 'Don't worry, I'm no candidate for the strip-tease cabaret.'

'Rowena!' Her mother flushed and looked away. She didn't even turn when Richard came through into the kitchen. He who was never punctual said, 'It's one o'clock, you know, Mother. Better get a move on. We should be having lunch.'

He pushed past Rowena, and began washing his hands in the water.

'Hey watch it!' Rowena hit him smartly across the knuckles with the egg spoon. 'Don't put your filthy hands in my clean water! Anyway, how the hell did you get in that state?'

'Just helping.'

Mary winced. 'Doing what exactly?'

'Unloading cement sacks.'

'How many?'

'About a dozen.'

'What on earth for?'

Richard shrugged.

'Have you not,' Rowena asked with bitter sarcasm, 'been admitted into our master's confidence?'

'As a matter of fact, I have.'

'Well, then?'

'It's a surprise. I promised John I'd keep it secret till he told you.'

There was a long uneasy silence.

'You mean,' Mary said heavily, 'that *you* share a secret with *them*, these gunmen, that *you* are going to keep from *us*, your family?'

'That's right,' Richard said, and impervious to her scandalized face, pulled out a chair at the kitchen table and glanced at the clock, a good boy taking his place for the first time punctually for lunch.

'Very nice . . . very nice, Mrs Greville!' Shaw spooned the last of his apricots into his mouth, pushed back his plate and smiled at her. 'Tomorrow has come!'

Standing at the sideboard, Mary looked at him and said nothing. The family had eaten in the kitchen. Now the three gunmen had lunched together in the dining-room, served by the women. 'It is the custom in my friends' lands,' Shaw had told her. Perhaps they were Mohammedans, she thought, but from where? This eating on their own was clearly intended to keep the family on a servile basis, but in fact Mary had greeted the arrangement with relief. The thought of sitting down and eating with them revolted her. It was bad enough serving them, being thrown scraps of remarks like this one.

'You have a saying, Mrs Greville . . . tomorrow never comes?'

She nodded.

'We have a saying . . . tomorrow with the apricots . . . but in our land, apricots do not grow. So – ' He shrugged his shoulders and smiled.

That was a clue, she thought. Where did apricots not grow? Turkey? The Sudan? Egypt? Pakistan?

'You have made our tomorrow come, Mrs Greville!'

He appeared to be in a good mood. There had been no interruptions all morning. The telephone had not rung once. Now he had eaten, he expanded further on the programme. The preparation of the cellar could wait until the morning. This afternoon, there was to be exercise, just as he had promised, in the 'lovely sunshine'.

It would be digging, as he had said. But Eleanor was to be excused. Too strenuous, unsuitable for her condition.

'See how considerate I am,' Shaw said when they all assembled in the back kitchen, dressed in their oldest clothes.

'At least, let me come out and watch,' Eleanor pleaded as if they were all going off into the garden to play croquet.

Shaw shook his head decisively. 'You must stay within. Someone is needed to answer the telephone.'

'It may not ring.'

'Equally, it may. Please do not argue.' He waved her back into the sitting-room. 'Naturally, you will not be alone. My colleague shall stay with you.' He nodded at the fawn-suited man who followed her like a dust-coloured shadow into the sitting-room and sat in the chair opposite.

'Do you trust him?' Ginny asked.

'As I would myself.'

'Big deal!'

'You are using sarcasm again. You are not endearing yourself to me.'

'I didn't mean to.'

Shaw came over to stand in front of her, legs apart, hands on his hips, the fingers of his right hand just lightly touching the Smith and Wesson under his coat. 'What *did* you mean then?'

'I want to know that Eleanor's all right.'

He turned round at Eleanor just visible through the sitting-room doorway flopped in one of the leather armchairs, holding a magazine in front of her, so that she didn't have to stare at her gaoler opposite.

'She is, I assure you, OK. Very OK! I will even let her have a window open.' He called something rapidly to the fawn-suited man, who shrugged and moved out of their line of vision. A draught of soft, heavily fragrant air drifted in from the garden.

Shaw swung round rapidly, and looked intently at Ginny as if expecting some reaction. When none came, his mouth tightened. He called, 'Come!'

He herded them in front of him. Then the red-haired Kuchi unbolted the back door, closing it again when they had all trooped out.

'Oh, how lovely!' Mary Greville sighed, putting her hand to her cheeks, as if to capture the warmth of the sun on her skin. 'It feels as if we've been shut in for life.'

'Less than twenty-four hours, Mrs Greville. Remember, some people *are* shut up for life.'

Shaw's words sounded reasonable enough. But the tone was not. Mary exchanged a quick, speaking look with Gordon, the kind they hadn't exchanged for years. Shut up for life? Him? For what? Murder? Maybe he'd been imprisoned in some other country, or maybe he'd been wrongly blamed, Mary thought. He'd been kind to Eleanor just now. He hadn't laid a finger on the girls. He seemed friendly to Richard, now bringing up the rear, and talking happily enough to him about tank battles. The houses at his school were named after famous generals. His was Montgomery, top house for the year, just beating Haig.

Then they rounded the corner of the house and Mary saw the pegs laid out between the garage and the old cellar door. They looked like the miniature wooden crosses with names on them that people used to stick around the War Memorial at Medbridge on Remembrance Day, commemorating the Fallen in two World Wars.

Shaw halted them. 'You remember, Mrs Greville, saying how narrow your drive was, cars could not turn round?'

Mary nodded.

'We found the same ourselves, so – '

Gordon said, 'I thought we were going to dig the beds.'

'Beds?'

'Flower-beds.'

Shaw shook his head. 'No, *this*.'

'Why?' Ginny breathed.

'I am telling you why. To leave you a commemoration of our visit.'

'We won't need one.'

'A place for the cars to turn.' Shaw turned his back on Ginny and smiled pleasantly at Mary. 'A turning circle. You exercise yourself by digging out the foundations. We shall do the rest.'

Mary gave a fair imitation of smiling pleasantly back. One of us is mad. Must be. 'Thank you.'

'Ground's heavy round here,' Gordon said doubtfully. 'Bit heavy work for the girls.'

'Much better than staying inside,' Rowena said.

'She is right. And none of you shall come to any harm.' He looked at Ginny.

'Better not.' She narrowed her eyes.

'Otherwise you would certainly kill me. Yes?'

'Yes.'

He pretended to shudder. Then, eyes still on Ginny, busied himself with the implements. He handed out spades to Richard and Gordon, a fork to Mary and a shovel to Rowena.

'For you,' he said coming over to Ginny, 'the wheelbarrow. Collect the earth which the others dig out. Take it through there – ' he pointed to the laburnum arch – 'and empty it behind the garage there.' He smiled. 'It is an easy job.' He reached out his hand and for the first time touched her arm. 'I am being favourable to you.'

For the last three hours, as he continued to dig, his eyes down on the clay and rubble of the widening and deepening trench, Gordon Greville had been wondering if he could manage it. In his hands now was a spade, certainly an offensive weapon. If only he could manoeuvre his way round behind Shaw and then . . .

But could he? There stood Shaw leaning against the garage wall, in the slight shade of the laburnum arch, his right hand staying inside his coat. If he made a sudden dive at the man, might not Mary or Ginny or Rowena get killed?

He who had always been clumsy, how could his aim be swift, unerring and true? Had he the strength to do it in one fell blow? Had he the conviction that it was right to use violence when none had actually been used against them? Had he the cunning to disguise his intentions? Above all, had he the courage?

'Your daughters are working harder than you, Professor Greville! Should you not be showing them a better example?'

He bent lower over his spade, dug out a spit of earth, then another and another.

'That is better! That is good.'

Perhaps we're *all* mad, Mary Greville thought. The whole family. There is such a thing as collective madness. Whole communities, whole families suffering from an intense in-growing neurosis.

One day, someone will come and find us dig, dig, digging away like maniacal gravediggers, and when they ask what we poor mad things are doing, we will answer, 'Men came, and said build ye a church here, no a turning circle . . . and so, we did it. We are Paul on the Road to Damascus.'

'For God's sake,' Ginny snapped sharply to Rowena. 'Mind what you're doing!' A spadeful of earth had missed the wheel-barrow and landed on her foot.

Shaw looked at her uncertainly, eyes narrowed. He appeared just on the point of saying something when Eleanor appeared at the open window with the fawn-suited man beside her, and in a voice that she attempted to keep normal called, 'Someone on the telephone for you, Ginny.'

'Who?'

'Simon, I think.'

Shaw signalled to Hamid to take over with the exercise, and followed Ginny inside.

'Who is this Simon?'

'A friend.'

'Of yours?'

'Naturally.'

'The one Hamid saw you with in the inn?'

She nodded. 'I'm surprised you don't know his life history.' She kicked off her muddy shoes, as if mud or anything else mattered, and went through the kitchen into the sitting-room.

Eleanor again sat in the leather armchair, looking at Shaw fearfully as if she might inadvertently have said something wrong. The receiver lay on its side on the table.

Shaw put his finger to his lips, enjoining absolute silence in the room. Tiptoeing, he moved softly ahead of Ginny, lifted the receiver with delicate care, and covered the mouthpiece with his left hand.

'Brevity and normalcy.' He nodded and handed her the receiver. He stood beside her with the muzzle of the Smith and Wesson not quite touching the side of her head. As she hesitated, struggling to steady her voice before speaking, carefully he parted the strands of her hair with the barrel of the gun in a nauseating, near-lover-like gesture.

'Hello, Simon.'

As soon as she spoke, Shaw cocked his head on one side, and froze like some wild animal listening to every word, every nuance.

'You're out of breath!'

Simon sounded like a voice from another world. Normal, easy, friendly. Was there still such a world beyond these walls?

'I've been hurrying.'

'That the only reason?'

Ginny saw the gunman frown. Immediately she said loudly, 'Of course it was.'

'All right. Just a joke, silly girl. Wondering if I . . .'

'No, of course not, I mean, yes.' Ginny shot the gunman a look of wild apology. He had put his free hand close to the telephone cradle, his forefinger poised above the bell bar. She gulped and steadied her voice. 'I was outside.'

'So Eleanor said.'

'Gardening.'

'That I don't believe.'

Immediately Shaw leaned across, seized the phone and covered the mouthpiece. 'I do not like *not believe*. Make him believe!'

'How did the judging go?'

'Bit of a sweat, but OK.'

'What about your own entries?'

Simon sighed. 'One second, one third. You should have come.'

'Sorry I couldn't make it.'

'Too lazy?'

'You know me.'

A pause. Softly, 'I'm not really sure I do.'

Dangerous ground. 'When did you get back?'

'Half past six. About five minutes ago.'

'Nice of you to ring straight away,' she said with finality.

'Guinevere?'

'Yes, Simon?'

'Am I bothering you?'

Shaw mimed to get rid of him.

'No, Simon. It's just that I'm . . . we're sort of madly busy . . .'

'I see. Doing what?'

'Extending the drive.'

'Fantastic!'

'Making a turning circle actually.'

'Come and have a drink. Sober yourself up.'

'When?'

'Now! This minute!'

The barrel of the gun pressed coldly on her scalp. 'I can't.'

'Why? Give me one good reason.'

Ginny glanced desperately at Shaw. He had moved the gun

away from her head. He pointed it now at the front door. Just clear of the trigger his forefinger moved up and down miming death, death, death to Simon if he came.

'There's only one reason,' Ginny said harshly into the mouthpiece. 'The real reason, Simon. I don't want to. Just don't want to. Simple as that.'

Simon replied in a curiously dignified tone, 'I see.'

Then Shaw put his finger on the cradle bell and severed the connection.

No one spoke. Ginny held the dead instrument in her hand till Shaw motioned her curtly to replace it. She trembled with a mixture of fear and misery. She had despised her mother this morning for her outburst after telephoning. But now she experienced the same intolerable strain. Her teeth chattered. She felt sick and cold. She felt degraded and treacherous for doing what Shaw had ordered.

'And now you are imagining that you have some sort of – ' Shaw hesitated and then sneered. 'Love. Sex love. For that bourgeois landowner.'

'Farmer. Earner of an honest living. No. I'm not.' She glared back into Shaw's bright hard eyes.

'Whatever he is – ' Shaw came right over to her and pointed the Smith and Wesson at her throat – 'if he comes here he will be a nothing. It will not be enough to send him away. He will not reach the door. He will be a dead man before he knocks. Hamid never misses.'

Ginny said nothing.

'Never shall you come to the telephone again! It is forbidden. If *he* asks for you, Rowena shall say you do not wish to speak with him.' Then Shaw strode to the window and shouted, 'Exercise is over! You shall all come in!'


Though the flowered cretonne curtains had been drawn tightly, Shaw had insisted that the sitting-room light should also be out. The only illumination came from the flickering kaleidoscope of the television round which the family and two of the gunmen were grouped in a semi-circle. Hamid was upstairs on watch at the landing window.

Supper was over, the washing-up done. Shaw had remained moody and for the most part silent, though there were odd bursts of attempted bonhomie. 'Recreation time!' he had called, bidding them come in to watch television like good children who had done their homework.

They were real television addicts, these gunmen, Ginny had noticed. Despite constant aircraft interference, the instrument was usually turned down, but rarely off. Though it was clear that Kuchi did not understand English, on his periods off watch he was always goggling into the box – Open University, Children's Hour, Watch with Mother, the cookery programmes – anything and everything appealed to Kuchi.

It was now the Nine O'Clock News – the worsening world economic situation, the famine in Ethiopia, violence on the Zambian border, strikes. A bank robbery in Hendon. Not clear exactly how much the thieves had got away with; but thousands, and much of it in gold. The murder on the M1. Three men were being sought in connection with the strangling of a girl hitch-hiker two days ago. There were Identikit pictures. Mary glanced nervously at Gordon. Then the pictures crackled as a jet came low over the house on the approach. Ginny got up quickly to adjust the set.

'Leave it! Stay where you are!' Shaw said sharply. 'Go sit down!'

And turning to Gordon, 'It will soon come all right. Yes?'

'Yes.'

Almost immediately the crackling ceased, the Identikit faces faded. The newscaster smiled. Pictures by satellite of the Queen arriving in Philadelphia, wearing a chic hat, carrying a bouquet of roses, smiling. A guard of honour, crowds in the streets in open-necked shirts and sleeveless dresses. Eleanor mopped her eyes.

Another jet came over, very low – the early night tourist flights coming home – the shriek of the engines drowning out the announcer's voice introducing 'our Diplomatic Correspondent'. Her Majesty returns on British Airways Echo Foxtrot, arriving at Grantwick on Monday.'

Northern Ireland. A boy of fifteen held in connection with the shooting of a soldier. Cricket. Surrey at the Oval. The tennis semi-finals at Wimbledon. A girl of thirteen attempting to swim the Channel. The News petered out, gave way to the Morecambe and Wise Show. Though Kuchi was totally absorbed, Shaw lost interest.

'Tomorrow we rise at seven-thirty.' Shaw surveyed them sternly, his eyes resting longest on Ginny. 'No laziness. Breakfast. Then clearing and furnishing the cellar.'

There was silence, broken by the strains of 'Give me sunshine' from the television. Then Mary said, almost as if she was speaking to a twelve-year-old child, 'Eleanor . . . bedtime.'

Eleanor immediately rose and like a sleepwalker made for the door. Ginny jumped up. 'I'll make her a hot drink.'

Both were allowed to leave the sitting-room. But while Eleanor went on her own up the stairs, Shaw followed Ginny into the kitchen. He stood just inside the door, watching her carefully as she went through into the larder for the tin of Ovaltine and the pitcher of milk.

Outside it was a bright clear night. All the stars were out. All in their same relative positions, the Plough, Pegasus, the North Star, she could see them well. Yet not one light from any house or neighbour. Only the walls of the thick-growing oaks and beech trees. No sign of Medbridge. No sign of Simon's house six miles away beyond the beech coppice and the hop gardens and the wheatfields.

Completely cut off. Imprisoned in another world. In an

alien land. Ginny shivered as she stepped back into the bright kitchen. She took out a milk pan from the cupboard. A strange feeling had come over her – she felt almost home-sick in the middle of her own home, in the bosom of her family, surrounded by all their familiar things.

'What is the matter with you?'

'Nothing.'

The blinds were down over the kitchen window. But beyond it would be the rosy pink glow in the northern sky over London. Within thirty miles of them lived ten million people. Yet, Ginny thought, as far as Fallowlands was con-cerned they were further away than Mars or Venus or the Milky Way. Further than anything living or tangible or finite. As far away, in fact, as the other side of the grave.

Gordon Greville descended the stone cellar steps with the slow reluctance of a man going into the condemned cell. He disliked cellars. He suffered from a secret childhood hang-up, the result of his father's aptitude for administering the most psychologically searing punishments.

Besides, he was carrying a mattress, and the steps were dangerously worn. Centuries of feet had hollowed them in the middle, so that now he came to think of it, they were shaped like neck-holds on a guillotine, and a damp chill struck up through the soles of his shoes as far as his ankle bones.

'Come, Professor Greville,' Shaw called from below. 'Our preparations will take all day at this rate! We must brisken our pace!'

The night had been uneventful. Shaw had collected the mail from the letter box at the end of the drive – mainly circulars, but there was a letter from Bill in New York for Eleanor. She was allowed to open it, and read it, but then had passed it over to Shaw for what he called 'censorship'.

There had been a phone call for Mary – an invitation to Sunday lunch-time drinks which she hastily refused.

Breakfast over, it was down to the cellar which despite its whitewash and its renovations smelled of mushrooms. An electric light with a naked bulb hung from the main centre beam. It peaked and distorted the faces of the two gunmen and the women, gave them all a hostile macabre quality.

'Put it on the truckle bed,' Mary said to him, flicking an invisible lock of hair from her forehead, the way she did only when she was near distraction. 'Surely you don't need any more?' she asked the gunman querulously. 'You've got three beds now. A table. Rugs. A radio. Books. Your friends can't read!'

Her voice rose. Shrill, accusative, near hysterical. Fastening on irrelevances, the way Mary did when she was at her wits' end. Poor Mary! If she would simply accept that the gunmen intended them no personal harm. They were making them break the law, yes. But that was all. He was sure now they were not those M1 murderers. They were only in hiding. Men in hiding did not draw attention to themselves by shooting off guns or assaulting people. He fully understood that the cellar was a refuge from detectives. If there was any sort of alarm out for these three in this area, Fallowlands might well get a visit from the Medbridge police. It was a sensible precaution.

But even as Gordon reasoned against Mary's doubts, he knew he was reasoning against his own. Medbridge police consisted of a sergeant who was about to retire with a young PC assistant, and their minds turned more on double-yellow-line parking and who threw the jumping cracker at the Noise Abatement meeting, than on arresting gunmen.

Besides, these arrangements were too elaborate, too thought out. Why the preparation of the cellar today? And why the digging of the turning circle? Were they really just trying to keep the family healthfully occupied? Or was there some much more sinister purpose?

In the coldness of the cellar, Gordon Greville struggled to maintain his belief in these men. To banish the dreadful fears and premonitions that lay beneath the surface of his reason. He had experienced a terrible certainty that here would be his grave, that here life would end for him. That here would be his final confrontation that all his life, with his mild liberalism, he had struggled to avoid. He was not a fighter. His father had tried to make him one, and failing, had hated him. All these fears and dreads dated back to that. There was good in all men, even these three. So far they had kept their promise. The ordeal was a third over and all the family were alive and well and unharmed.

'We need one more bed and mattress,' Shaw snapped his fingers at the red-haired man.

'You're wanted, Kuchi!' Rowena grinned in the silly, pert manner she used with these men.

'You can go with him, Richard. Help him.' Shaw smiled at the boy.

'Why more beds?' Ginny asked, her chin up, staring Shaw straight in the face, her eyes glittering hatred. She, too, in her own way, provokes him, Gordon thought.

'Because it may be necessary to take one of you as hostage with us.'

'In which case,' Gordon said heavily, 'as head of the family I must insist that the hostage be myself.'

Shaw laughed, throwing his head back so that his peaked shadow flitted over the whitewashed walls. 'Alas, you would probably be needed above! To send the police on their way.'

'Not necessarily. My wife could get rid of them.'

Shaw shook his head. 'Besides –' his eyes flickered from Rowena to Ginny – 'we would all prefer more amusing company. With respect, Professor. No offence, you understand.'

'You see,' Mary whispered, as they smoothed a rug

together. He is evil underneath. Evil!'

'Desperate more like, my dear.' Gordon straightened. He watched Shaw prowl round the uneven walls of the inner cellar, stare up at the single barred window, peering into the old bread oven and the meat store, step under the low vaulted arches that led to the unfloored, unlit part, disappearing into the darkness, so that one could imagine for a moment that it was all a bad dream.

Then he reappeared again, smiling. 'They are very thick the foundations, yes?'

'Ten feet in places. They used this as an air raid shelter in the war.'

'War?'

' 'Thirty-nine to 'forty-five.'

'Oh, *that*. It is a very long time ago. There have been many wars since.'

'True,' Gordon agreed. 'But not global.'

'Global.' Shaw contradicted him irritably.

'Don't argue with him!' Mary whispered. 'He doesn't like it. He frightens me when he looks like that.'

'And this door is stout, too,' Shaw called from the far end of the cellar. His voice echoed . . . stout, stout, *stout*.

'The same oak as for Nelson's ships,' Gordon replied in his lecture-room voice. 'Hard as iron.'

Richard came down the steps noisily, dragging the mattress from the spare-room bed behind him.

'Careful with that,' Mary said, fastening on unimportant things again, 'you'll tear the cover!' She arranged the chairs, the beds, the table, as though it was some guest-room. She even suggested to Shaw that there should be flowers, but he brushed the item aside.

'It is very nice, Mrs Greville. Very nice now! And as we have all worked so hard, we shall all have some coffee.'

'I'll go and make some,' Mary said. 'Come and help me Ginny, will you please?'

'No. You make the coffee. But she shall stay down here.'

Mary was aware of a shameful cowardly relief rising inside her with every step upwards out of the cool graveyard smelling of dampness and into the warmth of the sunshine upstairs. She knew she was being sent up alone with no guard because Shaw knew she would do nothing. She was too frightened to do anything but obey him to the letter. She tried to comfort herself by saying that nothing would happen to any of the family so long as they all did as they were told. She glanced at the familiar face of the kitchen clock. Five past ten. She heard the clink of bottles being set on the front step, the rattle of a metal basket. The milkman leaving the milk, picking out her note with the money, pencilling in his book. All so normal.

It was when she went to the sink that she saw the bulky shadow moving crosswise over the yard outside where she dried her washing. At first she thought it was the milkman. Maybe she hadn't left enough money. She panicked. Then a key turned in the empty lock. The latch rattled as someone shoved hard against the new stout bolts.

Then impatient knuckles hammered the panels. Before Mary had time to gather her shattered wits together, an angry voice shouted, 'Mrs Greville! It's me. Mrs Bristowe. And you've locked me out!'

'Something I've done wrong, is there?'

When Mary had unbolted the door, there stood Mrs Bristowe at her most formidable, prepared to take ever deepening umbrage. 'And why d'you trust me with a key if you bolt up against me?' She advanced a couple of paces, then stood with her stout knock-kneed legs apart, head lowered, big jaw thrust, small eyes darting around. A rhinoceros about to charge. Poor vulnerable lonely Mrs Bristowe! Mary had never felt so protective towards her. But all Mary could whisper was, 'How did you get here?'

'On the milk float.' Mrs Bristowe jerked her head behind her. A faint whine was all that remained as the milk float disappeared down the drive. 'Alf's relieving today. Lives up my way, does Alfie.' She breathed deeply, her big chest rising and falling with anger. 'Which is another thing . . .'

'Didn't you get my letter?' Cautiously, but with haste, Mary stepped sideways and backwards. Drew the cellar door softly shut behind her.

'What letter? I didn't get no letter! I saw what you left for Alfie. No milk. Holidays. You never said nothing about holidays neither.'

'I wrote to you,' Mary said in a low rapid voice.

'I got no letter.' Mrs Bristowe began unbuttoning her long fawn top coat that she wore all the year round. 'Was it telling me about your – ' Mrs Bristowe heaved out the word – 'holiday?'

'I wrote to tell you not to come.'

'I got no letter.'

'It was posted in time for the morning collection. I wrote to you not to come today.'

'For why?' Mrs Bristowe shrugged herself out of her coat, turned, and big bottom waggling reproachfully, hung the coat on the hook at the back of the door with a long-suffering sigh.

'Because I couldn't do with you. Not today. You shouldn't have come.' Mary spoke softly and urgently. There was not a moment to spare before getting rid of her.

'I'd have thought before a holiday you'd need me more than ever.'

'Not this one, *no*. Please, *please* do as I say!'

Mrs Bristowe had unzipped her plastic bag with a long-suffering air, and with awful unalterable purpose she extracted a clean overall and shook it free of its folds.

'Put it away!' Mary put her hand on the bag, but Mrs

Bristowe snatched it back.

'Please . . . *please* go!'

'Got someone else, have you? Someone a bit younger?' Tears, unnatural and pathetic, trickled down Mrs Bristowe's heavy face. 'Is that why you're talking all quiet? So your new lady help doesn't hear?'

'Mrs Bristowe – '

'Don't you want me no more?'

'But it's only for this week, Mrs Bristowe! Please understand. I want you next week. I mean the week after next . . .'

'There, you see! It's like I say.'

'No, it isn't. You see, it's our holiday.'

'First you've said of it to me.' Mrs Bristowe pursed her lips. 'Fine carry-on, I must say.' At a safe distance from Mary, she buttoned up her clean white overall.

'It was unexpected.'

Mrs Bristowe sniffed, half with tears, half in angry disbelief. Now she extracted from her bag a pair of Marks and Spencer's plastic pumps and, heavily breathing, began to unlace her walking shoes.

'No, don't take those off! You're going!' Mary snatched the shoes out of her hand and stuffed them back into the bag. 'You're going! Now come on! Please! Off you go!'

'There's no bus for another hour or more.'

'Walk then!' She put her hands on the big shoulders and pushed her round.

'That I won't! Why should I?' Mary felt the strong muscles. 'And you've no right to push me neither, that you haven't!'

'Just go. Go. Go!' Faintly but unmistakably, there came the sound of feet ascending the cellar steps. Gordon, Mary prayed, let it be Gordon. He'd get rid of Mrs Bristowe. Or Ginny, or Rowena or even Eleanor.

'If you don't want me no more . . . what about my money?'

'My bag's upstairs. I'll pay you next time.'

'Doesn't look to me – ' she spread her feet, trunklike legs taking root – 'as there'll be a next time.'

'All right . . . I'll get the money! You wait outside.' Mary took her arm to get her across the kitchen floor. Behind, in the back lobby, she heard the cellar door open, felt the draught of cool air on her bare legs, heard rapid footsteps, knew by the crafty look in Mrs Bristowe's eyes that it was Shaw who stood beside her.

'Aren't you going to introduce us?' he asked, smiling as Mary turned her head. Without taking his dark eyes off Mrs Bristowe's face, he stepped back and called something sharply upstairs to Hamid.

There was a flood of that same unintelligible language. Shaw listened with his head on one side, nodding. Then he looked back curiously at Mrs Bristowe.

'This is my help, Mrs Bristowe. The one, you remember, I wrote to . . .'

'I see.'

'And this is a friend of my husband's who's staying for a few days. Mr Shaw.'

'Pleased to meet you, sir.'

'Madame.' Shaw bowed and then smiled. 'Do I understand you arrived on the milk vehicle?'

'That's right.'

'How charmingly British and unexpected!'

'Mrs Bristowe is just going.'

'But she's only just arrived!'

'Even so,' Mary said desperately, 'she's going. She wants to go.'

'Where does she live?'

'Right the other side, sir. On my own. Got the old water-mill cottage.'

'Then can I give you a lift?'

'Oh, that would be ever so kind.' Mrs Bristowe beamed a

reproachful look on Mary. 'But I don't like to bother you, sir.'

'Not at all. It's a long walk to the village. And already it is hot.'

'Well,' Mary said uncertainly, 'I'll just slip upstairs and get your money, Mrs Bristowe.'

She began running up the stairs, as if for some reason time was vitally important. She was breathless by the time she reached the top. How silly of her to get into such a panic! There was nothing whatsoever to get into a state about. Mrs Bristowe had seen nothing untoward. Shaw had been understanding with her. Really quite charming. Clearly Mrs Bristowe had no suspicions whatever. Mary searched for her handbag, opened it, found her wallet and extracted the only money she had. Three pound notes. Then she went downstairs.

Everything was quiet. She walked through into the kitchen waving the notes. Shaw was sitting at the table, arms folded across his chest. He stood up when she came in, leaned forward and took the three pounds out of her hand. He laughed as he pushed them into his pocket. 'That is what you owe me.'

'Do I?'

'Yes.'

'Where's Mrs Bristowe?'

'She went on her way.'

'What about her money?'

'I paid her.' He tapped his pocket. 'I thought it safer lest you decided to write a message on the money.'

'I wouldn't have dreamed of it!'

'A joke! That is all. I'm sure you are sensible. I gave her an extra pound to save me getting out the Land-Rover.' He smiled. 'It seems there is a back way through the woods.'

'Yes.'

'So she was well content.'

'Good.' Mary ran her hands through her hair, tried to

remember what she'd come here to do, feeling suddenly quite weak with fright and the near-disaster of the last fifteen minutes.

'You were going to make some coffee, Mrs Greville!'

'So I was.'

Still distracted, she put the kettle on the stove, murmuring more to herself than to him, 'Well, I don't suppose I'll ever see her again!'

Shaw said sharply. 'What was that you said?'

'Mrs Bristowe. She's offended with me. She'll never come back to Fallowlands.'


'Mrs Bristowe will soon get over it. She likes working here. You mark my words, Mary, when all this is over, she'll come back.'

Gordon was markedly cheerful as they and the two girls filed back into the sitting-room when afternoon exercise was over. It was six forty-five and still warm.

'You all look exhausted.' Eleanor put down her magazine. 'Where's Richard?'

'Helping Shaw put away the garden implements,' Gordon said.

'Quite the senior prefect these days.' Ginny threw herself on the sofa. 'I must say, I could use a drink.'

'There's plenty of water in the tap,' Gordon smiled.

'And squashes.' Mary stretched her feet in front of her, luxuriously.

'Well, I'll fetch us all a jugful.'

'I mean something stronger,' Ginny said, closing her eyes. She looked very white round the lips, Mary thought, the pallor contrasting strangely with her sunburned forehead and cheekbones. Of all of them she was taking this invasion the most hard. Not in histrionics or weeping but within herself. 'I could do with a couple of brandies.'

'He's got the key of the drinks cupboard.' Eleanor nodded towards Hamid, sitting in his favourite place behind the front door.

'Where's Kuchi?' Rowena asked her.

'Up aloft.'

'Landing window?'

'I think so. He went up to your room while you were out. Took another of those hessian parcels in. Something quite long. Looked – ' Eleanor giggled weakly – 'like half a tent.'

'You know – ' Gordon returned from the kitchen with a jugful of squash and some paper picnic cups – 'you might just have hit on something, Eleanor. Maybe that's it. Those parcels are their worldly possessions. They've no suitcases, you notice?'

'That's true.' Mary drank the lemon squash gratefully and perked up. 'And why shouldn't they carry their stuff like that? Sensible really.'

'Maybe they do usually live off the land,' Rowena said. 'Camp out. Soldiers of Fortune.'

'Misfortune,' Ginny said, her eyes still closed.

'Those parcels could contain tents, clothes and cooking utensils,' Gordon said slowly.

'Or bombs, handgrenades and machine-guns.'

'Now, now, Guinevere!'

'Don't call me that.'

'Ginny then. Cheer up.'

'They could be a body, couldn't they?' Eleanor said. 'They haven't found those men for the M1 murder yet.'

'It's not bits of body. Something metal. Nothing soft,' Rowena said.

'Valuable. Otherwise why keep my room locked?'

'Well, we're near the half way mark. No harm's been done.' Gordon said, 'And Shaw was remarkably decent to Mrs Bristowe this morning.'

'I tell you,' Mary sighed, '*I* couldn't get rid of her. But he was so nice. Firm, but nice.'

'There, drink up, Ginny. You'll feel much better. Ah,' he changed his tone warningly as Shaw came through from the back lobby, 'we are just having a lemon squash, Mr Shaw. Will you join us?'

'Presently, thank you.' Shaw was all smiles. 'But I had already planned in my mind a small celebration. For the successful and amicable half way as you might put it.' He snapped his fingers at Hamid and pointed to the drinks cupboard. Obediently Hamid rose, glided over and handed him the key.

'What will you all have?' He spread his hands, the genial host. 'Anything you like. Even – ' a roguish smile – 'Rowena.'

'Where's Richard?' Mary Greville asked anxiously.

'Washing his hands like a good boy. You fret too much, Mrs Greville. Now what shall I pour for you?'

'Sherry, please. Nothing for Eleanor, squash is best for her.'

'But this is an occasion, Mrs Greville.'

'I prefer the lemon squash, thanks,' Eleanor said coldly.

'And I'll have a brandy,' Ginny sat up straight and opened her vivid blue eyes at Shaw.

'Sherry for me,' Gordon said heartily, intercepting Ginny's bitter look and sighing.

'There.' Shaw poured the drinks and brought them round to each of them, bowing and smiling broadly. 'We will all drink to our continuing friendship.' He raised a glass to his lips. 'So far it has been so good, yes? We are still all well. We are still smiling. Never – ' he slipped his fingers under his jacket and touched the holster – 'have I had to use this.'

'No.' Gordon sipped his drink and smiled warmly back. 'I'm beginning to have a suspicion that your bark is a good deal worse than your bite.'

'Your pardon?' Shaw said, his smile slightly narrowing. 'Bark? Bite?'

'Oh, nothing,' Gordon said heartily. 'Just means that you're a good deal less ruthless than you try to make out.'

'Do tell me, Mr Shaw,' Ginny murmured fifteen minutes later. 'How did you manage to get rid of Mrs Bristowe?' She was drinking her second brandy. The white pallor had faded from around her mouth. There were two bright spots of colour in her cheeks. Her eyes glittered very blue against them. She looked devastatingly, heartbreakingly beautiful.

'Ah.' Shaw smiled. His good humour was continuing to hold. 'That was easy.' He tapped his pocket. 'Money.'

'Money?'

He smiled. 'The great solver of all problems.'

'How much did you give her?'

'Four pounds. Too much you will say. But she is lonely. She lives alone. No relatives. No friends. It is very sad.'

Gordon exchanged a comfortable look with Mary.

'Did you also pay her for her coat?'

'What coat?' Shaw's eyes hardened.

'That fawn one of hers.'

'She had no coat.'

'I saw it behind the kitchen door after she'd gone.'

'Are you sure?' Gordon put down his glass.

'Of course I'm sure.' Ginny was looking steadily at the gunman. 'I'm also sure she'd never leave it behind.'

'I didn't see it,' Gordon said.

'Nor did anyone else, Professor. Your daughter, this daughter, tries hard to make trouble. Where no trouble is. Where all is happy. She needs a man to teach her.'

The good mood had cracked. Now he came and stood in front of Ginny – swaggering, threatening, legs apart, hands on hips. And while he mimed his threats, he called something over his shoulder softly but furiously to Hamid.

'She's tired,' Gordon said. 'This afternoon was exceptionally hot. Hard work too.'

'Not hard enough,' Shaw snapped. 'It is her mother who can be tired. She is young.'

'Hard,' Gordon repeated.

'Oh, I'm all right.' Mary flushed.

'Nevertheless, you shall rest, Mrs Greville. Go – ' he stabbed his finger almost into Ginny's eyes, smiled briefly when she flinched. 'Get supper, miss. I am hungry. Nor do I want cold ham again from your refrigerator. I want something hot. Properly cooked. In the deep freeze, there are chops. We will have lamb chops.'

For a moment, Ginny sat exactly where she was, staring up at Shaw.

'Go and get them!'

At first Gordon thought she was going to refuse, make a scene. He came out in a cold sweat. But then she seemed to think better of it. She shrugged, gave Shaw a furious, defiant look, and then went off into the outer kitchen.

Then a small silence. Then the screaming began. Ginny screaming and sobbing as he hadn't heard her do since she was a tiny child. He jumped up. He couldn't remember crossing the kitchen floor. But he could remember pushing past Shaw when he tried to stop him.

Ginny was over by the window, half kneeling, half slumped to the floor. She had one hand clapped at her ear, as if the screaming belonged to someone else, her forehead pressed to the white side of the freezer, one hand draped over the top as if she'd been trying to pull something out and then fallen.

He went to clasp her hand, to raise her up. Then his eye was caught, riveted, by the huge white bulk in the freezer. His senses spun. He leaned forward, shuddering. He saw Mrs Bristowe's huge body clad still in her white overall painfully bunched up, eyes open, glazed and frozen and protruding like cod's eyes. A rime of white on her brows and her frizzy hair, an imitation Santa Claus, face mottled red and blue and patchily yellow. Hideous! Dreadful! Not real at all. Some figment of Ginny's disordered imagination passed to him. They were all going mad, seeing strange shapes out of harmless things. Legs of mutton, bacon, chickens. There was a wire or a string or something round her throat. Dried frozen Oxo-coloured blood oozed from the side of her mouth.

'You see, Professor . . . it is not good to say,' Shaw's voice whispered softly behind him, 'that I am less ruthless than I try to make out. Or that I bark like a house dog but do not bite.'

# descent approved

At first, Mary Greville cut them without thinking. All red flowers that her scissors could find in the garden – dahlias, poppies, phlox, verbena – snipping away madly at the blood-coloured blossoms. Not that there had been much blood. Who would have thought there would have been so little, she thought, paraphrasing Macbeth, a bubble of hysterical laughter rising in her throat like phlegm. Just one spot at the corner of Mrs Bristowe's mouth and the rest of her cold and dead as mutton. Oh, my God! She put the back of her gloved hand to her mouth to stifle her thoughts. Behind her, silent as a shadow, Hamid followed. From aster to rose-bed. From berberis bush to polyanthus border, his feet making no more than a faint brushing sound on the dry lawn.

They were maniacs, of course. Now she knew. She would never believe in their word again, no matter what Rowena and Richard had said. Who would have thought that *they,* her own flesh and blood, would have taken Mrs Bristowe's murder so quietly? Children were odd these days. The younger, the worse, the more hardened to violence. There was violence all over the world. Youngsters were conceived and born and nurtured in it, as Gordon said. Fed it on television, in the newspapers, in daily living. But Rowena of all people. Rowena who would weep over a dead rabbit, not to show the slightest sorrow for Mrs Bristowe! She was fascinated by Shaw, of course. The adolescent girl, the susceptible one. Richard she could understand. Richard was his grandfather all over again. He had even tried to explain the murder to his mother. Shaw had had no option. *No option.* Mrs Bristowe would never have kept her mouth shut. Oh God, in such a world of what use to pray for peace?

Mary Greville must have let out some exclamation of anguish, for Hamid came close to her, his expression alert, suspicious. She indicated the thorns on the roses, pretended she had pricked her finger. They were huge this year, those thorns. There were pale pink thornless ones over by the lily-pond but she wanted none of those. There was a brilliant red Britannia rhododendron in the shrubbery, the colour of a railway signal set at danger, she snipped it off and put it in her basket. Crimson berberis, thick with prickles, a peony as big and firm as a cabbage. Armful of love-lies-bleeding. There were some scarlet geraniums at the back of the house, but she did not feel strong enough yet to go round there. The gunmen had buried Mrs Bristowe in the turning circle. Shaw wouldn't admit it, but she knew they had. She had heard them shovelling what sounded like cement after they had gone to bed, the scrape of spades. A lucky coincidence for the gunmen that the grave was ready. Or was it a coincidence? Wasn't it all part of the plan? And was not the grave, if grave it was, too big for only one?

'Those are very beautiful flowers you have there, Mrs

Greville,' Shaw said pleasantly as she stepped back into the kitchen, through the back door just as Mrs Bristowe had done almost exactly twenty-four hours ago. He looked down at her trug full of flowers and foliage.

She nodded. After last night she couldn't bring herself to speak to him.

The smile faded. He thinks we are being unreasonable, she thought, the hysterical laughter bubbling up again.

'You will be quick with your business at the church. I shall expect you back by one.'

She shrugged, stripped off her gardening gloves, put them away in the drawer. She took out two blocks of Oasis.

'What are those for?'

'To hold the flowers.'

He ushered her through the house to the front door. Hamid had already brought the family Vauxhall round.

'You may drive,' Shaw said to her. 'Your licence is in order? Your tax? I do not want you stopped by the police.' Politely he opened the driver's door for her, waited till Hamid had settled himself into the passenger seat. 'If you are spoken to by anyone, you will be discreet.' He slammed the door. 'You will remember Mrs Bristowe.'

It took several seconds before she could steady her nerves sufficiently to get the car into gear and pull away. She drove jerkily down the drive to the lane at the bottom. Hamid glanced at her suspiciously, as if this were some trick to discompose him, then shrugged and kept his eyes on the road, still hooded behind the dark glasses.

She waited before turning into the lane, trying to get her courage up. She kept fearing that something would come hurtling round the corner, and there would be an accident. Then the police would come and by the time she got home, Shaw would have killed all her family.

When she did pull out, she drove as slowly as a hearse. It smelled like one, too, with all the flowers. All around her the familiar landscape looked strange. As if she'd been away on a long journey.

She parked by the Village Hall, and got out. As she walked to the lych-gate, she was aware of Hamid following her at a discreet distance. Then, just as she thought the coast was clear, round the corner on a collision course came Mrs Thurtle, Chairwoman of the Women's Institute.

'No, I can't come to the "Women for Peace service",' Mary said immediately. 'We're off on holiday.'

'What fun! Lucky you! Family well?'

'Marvellous, thank you. And yours?'

'As well as can be expected. Reginald feels the heat.' She looked doubtfully at the flowers in the big trug. 'What colourful flowers!' And then quickly, as though to get away from the subject, 'I hear your son-in-law's on the Royal Flight.'

Mary nodded, moving nervously away.

'A great honour. And a great responsibility.'

Hamid had stopped just inside the churchyard, stood reading the inscriptions on the gravestones. He followed her into the eleventh-century church, knelt in the pew nearest the pulpit and began to pray – all the time watching Mary closely from behind hands that piously covered his face.

What did he fear, Mary asked herself. A note tucked in a hymnal? A chalked message on the Crusader's tomb at her feet? Writing on the vestry wall?

When she went through to the vestry to fetch her jug of water from the verger's tap, Hamid rose to his feet, turned himself, though there was no one there to question him, into the tourist again. Looking up at the raftered ceiling, sliding his hands over the choir stalls as he followed her like a cat, taking up his kneeling position again when she returned.

Mary didn't pray. She was too frightened to form words. But she took up her basket of blood-red flowers to the altar, wordlessly demanded of the pale-blue-clad glass shepherd with his flock in the east window that He *do something*.

Then she spread the newspapers on the floor in front of the altar and began.

Last week's arrangement was still fresh and pretty. The fluted side vases each held three pale yellow carnations, two sprays of sweet-scented forsythia. The centre bowl a fragile dainty cloud of cream rosebuds and maidenhair fern. Speaking the Word of the Lord by the wonders of His Creation. Reverent and gracious. Saying it with flowers.

Mary whipped them out and tossed them on to the newspaper. Into those dainty silver side vases she stuffed the huge dark red roses with their half-inch thorns. In between them she put long spikes of berberis, their tiny crimson flowers shrunk to drops in the sharp prickles of their stems. The centre bowl she made into a mound. She put the blocks of Oasis on top of one another. In a frenzy of speed and zeal, she prodded in the rhododendrons and the red trumpets of the gloxinia. She stripped the love-lies-bleeding of its leaves. There must be no softening of green. Red, red, *red*. Red for danger, red for – for the blood which is shed for thee to preserve thy body and soul into everlasting life. Well, the blood bled right over the altar. The pointed droopy red flowers cascaded over the satin-embroidered altar cloth. She surmounted the arrangement with the big red cabbage of a peony. Surely they would see! They that have eyes to see, dear glass shepherd Lord, let them see!

And they that have ears to hear . . . she had flowers and to spare. Over the front of the pulpit, she spread her message. Roses stuck into the discreet wire mesh that was only used for weddings and harvests. Asters and red daisies and geraniums bursting from the lectern.

They had come here four hundred years ago to light the bonfires and sound the bell for the Armada. For the French wars. To take cover in the Battle of Britain. There was a Memorial window to the Few in the Lady Chapel overlooking the shallow valley where the Spitfires intercepted and the

Heinkels used to jettison their bombs. She put her last roses on the sill beneath it. She was lighting her glowing bonfire. Oh God, let them see!

She was on her knees in front of the altar rolling up the newspaper when the steeple clock chimed out noon. Hamid uncovered his face, rose to his feet, jerked his head for her to leave. She followed him meekly, the rolled newspaper under her arm. She was half way up the nave when the west door opened.

'Ah, Mrs Greville!' the Rector materialized out of the chequered sunlight. 'Busy as always. I hoped to catch you, though. I hear you're off on holiday. Won't be able to come to the Peace service after all your work. Anyway, our good wishes for – '

About to make his obeisance, his half-lowered reverent eye was caught by the riot of ghastly lurid red. Mary glanced over her shoulder. Against the white of the candles, the pale gold of the altar cloth, the whole dreadful arrangement screamed, yelled, stretched out its spiked arms to proclaim surely 'Murder!'

'Dear lady,' he murmured, 'it is Women for Peace,' shook his head at her artistic ineptitude, genuflected and went on his way.


Eleanor woke half way through the night. Something more than a vague physical malaise had disturbed her. She had been dreaming again, of course – the way she did when Bill was away – that she heard his voice and that they were together again. She sighed, half asleep. It had been such a lovely dream. Now she remembered it, hugging it to her against the present awfulness of reality.

She lay flat on her back, staring up at the paler darkness of the ceiling. All she could hear now was her mother and sisters' regular breathing. Muted country sounds of nightjars and owls, the bark of a dog fox. She wished she could go back into her dream, had reached for the bottle of sedatives, when she heard that high, thin noise again. Except that it was now more clearly defined. She dropped her outstretched hand and sat up. Extraordinarily, the dream came back. She heard voices, far away at the back of her mind. That same unhurried but clipped exchange of men's voices.

Confused, she shook her head to shake the sleep out of it. Slowly, she pushed back the clothes, swung awkwardly out of bed, and padded with caution past Rowena, who slept as lightly as a cat.

Eleanor had no clear theory in her mind. Pregnancy produced strange aberrations. In the enforced absence of their ordinary life, she longed fiercely for her husband's presence. But now, with all this horror, she felt she would wilt and die without him. She had almost persuaded herself by the time she reached the door that the crackling voices were her mind's expression of her whole being's need. She put her ear against the crack of the door. The voices grew louder. An aircraft's jets screamed directly overhead, almost drowning them out. Back they came again, as the aircraft swept over and away . . .

Rowena stirred in her sleep, muttered something about, 'But then Kuchi's a fool.' Fearfully, Eleanor turned the door knob. It moved quietly. No one stirred. She drew the door inwards no more than a finger width. The voices increased unmistakably in volume. She put her eye to the opening.

The landing was empty. A single 60-watt bulb lit the green carpet down the corridor to Rowena's room. There a bright frame of light rimmed the door. Voices came from behind it. She heard the sound of movement. Someone scraped what sounded like a chair. Eleanor pulled the bedroom door wider open and listened. There was the howl of something like a volume selector being turned up. She heard further staccato exchanges.

'. . . Clipper Five Six . . . over the Outer Marker . . .'

'Any delays for Seven Forty One? . . . Flight level one niner course two niner . . . descent approved.'

Then the sound of steps. Hamid coming back up the stairs. Eleanor drew in her breath sharply. She shut the door as quietly as she could. She stood for a moment leaning against it. Her teeth chattered, her whole body shook. Then she dragged herself away lest her uncontrollable shaking rattled the old door on its hinges and alerted Hamid, now just outside. She staggered towards Ginny's bed, and grasped her sister's bare shoulder.

'Ginny! Wake up! For God's sake!'

'What's up?' It was Rowena who woke first.

'Aren't you well?' Mary switched on the bedside lamp.

'Put it off!' Ginny sat up and ran a hand through her hair. 'Don't give those yobs any excuse to come in.' She brought out a torch from under her pillow, shielded the cone of light with her fingers. 'Sit down, Eleanor. It isn't urgent, is it? You haven't got violent pains or anything?'

Slowly Eleanor subsided on to the end of Ginny's bed. The trembling had stopped, but her body felt a mountain of dead cold weight. Her mind was numb, her spirits as heavy as lead.

'No, I'm all right.'

'What, then?' Ginny brought the torch beam nearer to Eleanor's face. Her shielding fingers shone bloody over the light. 'Did you have a nightmare?'

'I thought I had a dream,' Eleanor spoke slowly. 'Then it wasn't a dream. I heard voices. From across the landing. I went and listened.'

'You shouldn't have done.' Mary had got out of bed and now stood over her, brooding and helpless. 'They might have seen you . . .'

'What were they doing?' Rowena cautiously tiptoed across and knelt on Ginny's bed. They all four drew their heads close together, talking in whispers. 'Quarrelling?'

'No. Nothing like that.' Her mouth was dry. She licked her lips, speaking slowly. 'They've got some sort of radio in there. In your room, Rowena.'

'So?' Ginny asked.

'It's not an ordinary radio. They're picking up the aircraft. The ones going in to Grantwick.'

In the shielded torchlight, she looked around at their peaked, upshaded faces.

'What are you trying to say?' Mary asked.

'They're just listening in to aircraft, that's all, Mother dear,' Rowena whispered.

'But not just to pass the time of day,' Ginny said sharply.

'They've probably put a bomb on board one of them,' Eleanor said, her voice rising. 'Or . . . or they're going to!'

'Sssh! How could they? They've never left here.'

'They'll have friends. Accomplices.'

'Perhaps they're expecting a friend to land,' Mary said, darting an anxious look at Eleanor's ashen face.

'Complete with another batch of illegal immigrants, Mother dear?'

'Try to get to sleep now. Eleanor,' Mary said. 'There's nothing we can do about it. Get some rest. We'll try to talk to your father tomorrow. See what he makes of it.'

It was not much of a comfort, but it was all she had to offer.

By the light of the torch, Mary and Rowena scrambled back into their beds. Ginny still sat up, her knees drawn up under her chin, clasping her hands round her legs.

From her own bed, Mary watched her. It was a long time before Ginny put out the torch, and it was a long time after that before Mary herself drifted off to an uneasy sleep.

When she awoke again, it was with terrifying abruptness. The bedroom was full of pain and crying.

'Eleanor! My God, Eleanor!' Mary switched on the lamp and leapt out of bed. 'Eleanor!' She said her daughter's name over and over again. 'Eleanor.' She put her hand on her forehead. 'Eleanor, lovie,' crooning at her, as if she were a child. Eleanor's whole body squirmed from side to side in a spasm of pain. Mary saw the bloodstain spreading on the rumpled sheet. 'She'll have to have a doctor,' she said, straightening. 'I don't care what they say!'

She swept Ginny and Rowena aside, wrenched open the door, was past Hamid before he had time to grab her arm, tried the handle of the door of Rowena's room, and finding it locked, hammered and hammered and hammered at the thick oak panels with her fists.

'I am, Mr Greville, as you know, a very reasonable man.' Shaw stood in front of the sofa, addressing himself to Greville's bowed head, clasped in his hands. Gordon had become an old man in the last eight hours, Mary thought. She sat close beside her husband on the sofa, staring up at the gunman's amused face. 'If there were anything reasonable to be done – ' Shaw snapped his fingers – 'then like that it would be done. My colleagues and I . . .'

'You know damned well there is something you could do!' Gordon raised his head and glowered up at Shaw. He banged his clenched fists on his thighs. He drew in a deep breath to steady his voice and asked hoarsely, 'Let me get a doctor for Eleanor. *Now.*'

'Please, Mr Greville, that is *not* reasonable. Do not let us go over the tedium of the last half hour's argument. That is quite beyond reasonableness.'

'Why?' Mary demanded. 'Why is it unreasonable? Why?'
'Because I say it is.'
'It's a matter of simple humanity.'
'Ah, humanity, yes.' Shaw smiled to himself. He shook

his head impatiently while one of the early afternoon press of summer holiday jets screamed overhead. Mary sighed. The worry and misery over Eleanor's miscarriage had overshadowed the previous events of last night – Eleanor's dream and her hearing of the aircraft R/T. What the gunmen were up to had become of secondary importance. Except that they had indirectly caused Eleanor's miscarriage, not a doubt of it. But she could think of nothing now, except Eleanor's survival . . .

'I would personally be your hostage,' Gordon said as the aircraft engines died away.

Shaw tapped his gun. 'But you are already, with respect, my hostage, Mr Greville. You are not offering me anything. You are not talking sense. Any time I care to say so, like that – ' he snapped his fingers again – 'my colleagues would take you down to the cellar and shoot you.'

'So the cellar *is* for us,' Gordon said heavily. 'I thought it might be.'

'It is for whatever I say it is. *When* I say it is.'

There was a long-drawn-out pause. Birds twittered in the creeper beside the tightly closed windows. Rowena was clattering the lunch dishes in the kitchen. There were snatches of pop music from Ginny's radio up in Eleanor's room. The normal safe sounds of an English summer afternoon.

'You wouldn't dare,' Mary said. 'You'd never get away with it.'

The gunman smiled.

'And anyway, it wouldn't be worth your while.'

Shaw took out his gun and looked at it lovingly. 'No, that is true. Not at present.'

Gordon put a hand on her arm to stifle Mary's frightened exclamation.

'The doctor,' he persisted, 'I would guarantee he saw *nothing.*'

'How? Would you bandage his eyes?'

'No. But you could all stay out of sight.'

'What if he ordered her to hospital?'

'She could go. She would say nothing.'

'Nothing? Nothing? You know nothing, *old man*,' the gunman spat out contemptuously.

'Well, just let the doctor come and see her. We won't let her go anywhere. We'll make some excuse. One can always refuse. It's one's right. I'll promise you he will come and go and everything will be normal.'

'Normalcy, yes. But no longer is it *quite* normalcy. We progress a little beyond normalcy.'

'What the hell do you mean?'

Shaw's smile deepened. He shook his head. 'I do not wish to explain.'

'All right, don't. But let me phone the doctor.'

'I say it is unnecessary and too late. Too late for us. Too late for you. The foetus is dead.'

Mary closed her eyes. She had wrapped it in folds of newspaper into a bundle, the way she had wrapped the withered altar flowers in the church. She had put it quickly outside the bedroom door, out of Eleanor's sight, and when she had gone a little while afterwards on to the landing to get Eleanor a drink, the bundle had gone. The gunman had thrown it, she was sure, under a shovelful of cement, beside Mrs Bristowe's body in the turning circle trench.

'So,' Shaw smiled, 'it is now of no importance.'

'There's Eleanor. She's ill,' Mary said.

Shaw looked at Mary with sudden venom. 'You are soft. Spoiled. Decadent. There are thousands, millions, like that die all the time. Every year.' He walked up and down in front of them, gesticulating, working himself up into a frenzy. 'And women, your kind – ' he pointed with his gun at Mary – 'come here, this country, pay much much money to have done what has happened to your daughter.'

Gordon clasped his hands together in an exhausting effort

of self-control. 'Nevertheless,' he spoke quietly, 'as far as we're concerned, here and now, Eleanor needs medical care. Immediately. You must understand that.'

'She will survive. Women are strong. They are made to survive.'

A faint creak from the head of the stairs made Shaw spin round, his gun ready.

Ginny was slowly descending the stairs, carrying Eleanor's untouched lunch tray in her hands. Her face seemed to glow an incandescent white like the magnolia blossoms on the staircase window-sill. Her hair, loose to her shoulders, glittered in the broken shaft of sunlight splintered by the diamond panes. She wore her tight velvet pants and a low cut blouse of thin cotton. Shaw's eyes never left her. His expression subtly altered.

'Women,' he said, still staring at Ginny, 'can survive much.'

'If anything happens to Eleanor,' Ginny replied in a tone Gordon had never heard her use before, as if she could communicate with Shaw on a level of hatred unplumbed by them, 'I will personally kill you.'

'With what? How?' Shaw laughed, an ominous, amused delight mingling now with his venom. 'With your little hands?'

Ginny shrugged her bare shoulders, but didn't answer. When she reached the bottom of the staircase, she put down the tray on the hall table and with the same deliberate unhurried movements walked into the sitting-room, and past the sofa where her parents sat.

'Eleanor's temp's over a hundred,' she said quietly, and before Shaw had time to realize what she was doing, reached the phone and picked up the receiver.

'Put that down!' With one swift stride, Shaw stood in front of Ginny, his revolver in his hand. They heard the click of the safety catch.

'Don't, don't, don't,' Mary implored. But whether to Shaw or Ginny or both of them, she didn't know.

Deliberately Ginny bent her head. A lock of her hair fell over her face as she stretched out her hand and began dialling.

There was a loud bang. Mary screamed and buried her face in Gordon's shoulder. And then almost immediately she looked up again.

Shaw had knocked the receiver out of Ginny's hand with the butt of his revolver. He had seized her wrist in his left hand and twisted her arm round the back of her body. He was staring down into her face, the rest of them forgotten. His neck was arched, the veins standing out, his lips were drawn back from his teeth, his expression baleful. Ginny's eyes held his, matched them, mocked them. It was a battle

'I should kill you,' he hissed.

He gave another twist to her wrist, then released her abruptly. With his eyes still on her face, and with deliberation, he seized the top of her blouse and ripped it down. Ginny didn't try to stop him. She looked neither surprised nor disgusted. She simply smiled. An alien triumphant smile.

Gordon jumped to his feet. Shaw turned round contemptuously. 'Upstairs,' he gestured with his gun. 'Both of you. Come on. Move. Go to your poor sick daughter. I will deal with this one for you, have no fear.'

Half an hour later, Mary heard the ratcheting sound of the telephone dial. And about an hour after that, Ginny appeared in the bedroom doorway. She was wearing a smock over her velvet pants. She looked pale but tidy and completely composed. 'How's Eleanor?'

'Asleep. She looks terribly flushed, though.' Mary shrugged helplessly.

'I'm going down to the surgery to pick up a prescription. I've phoned. It'll be waiting.'

Gordon said nothing. He avoided looking at Ginny.

'I'm glad,' Mary said softly, looking across at Eleanor's bed, 'that you got Shaw to change his mind.'

At six-fifteen, just before the late-night chemist was due to close, Ginny drove the car rapidly in the direction of the village. Shaw sat beside her. He was dressed in jeans and T-shirt. Behind the small windows of the car, to the casual observer, he looked an ordinary young man out with his girl.

Ginny drove with detached competence. An iron door within her subconscious mind had slammed on the events of the last few hours. She had no feelings, no conscience, no emotions. Nothing. A steel computer had taken over. It moved her eyes, her hands, her feet. It was programmed to get her safely to achieve her reward of the bargain, the penicillin and the pain-killers for Eleanor and the safe, quiet return with it to Fallowlands.

The computer also assembled facts. It noted Shaw's silence. It noted his added venom towards her. It noted the way he turned in his seat at the bottom of the drive to stare back at the house, as if checking it carefully for normalcy.

Why?

Why are they listening to the R/T of aircraft using Grantwick? Were they expecting reinforcement? And if so, for what?

Half way to the village Shaw wound down his window. It was a warm heavy evening. The air was sweet with the smell of honeysuckle and the first crop of hay. But it was not for that. It was the better to watch a 707, banking on the turn, low in the circuit, its belly rosy in the rays of the sun beyond the horizon. With an abrupt, peremptory wave of his hand, he signalled her to slow down, watching like a cat does a bird as the aircraft lowered itself into the layers of cloud, and disappeared beyond the tree-tops. Were they going to put a bomb on board an aircraft leaving Grantwick? Was that what they were doing up in Rowena's room? Making the thing? Or the timing device?

As Ginny turned the car at the corner stores and continued up into the High Street, Shaw draped a nonchalantly affectionate arm round the back of her seat. Unnecessarily as it happened, because the High Street was empty.

'Is that the chemist?' He indicated the big glass windows of the double-fronted old-fashioned shop.

'Yes.'

He surveyed it carefully, expertly.

'Then turn the car round and park over there.'

He pointed to the empty forecourt of the shuttered forge, almost directly opposite.

'I can see every move you make. You know what I will do if you try to give warning.' Politely he got out and opened the car door for her.

Unhurriedly she waited for a van to go by and then crossed the High Street. A woman was pushing a pram and looking in the closed shop windows, otherwise the street was deserted. The chemist's display window was full of bathing caps and sun tan oil. It was unbelievable, frivolous almost, that people still bothered.

There was only one customer in front of her. A middle-aged man, a farm worker by the look of him, with a bandaged hand.

'Awkward when it's your right,' he said, holding up his hand as they waited for the chemist to reappear from the dispensary at the back.

The computer made Ginny nod sympathetically, ask, 'How did you do it?'

'Baling. The governor ran me to the surgery.'

She nodded again, turned away to break the conversation, aware of the eyes watching her from across the street.

'Yours is ready, miss.' The chemist came through from

the dispensary.

'Don't mind, do you, sir, if I serve this young lady while I let your lotion stand?'

The man shook his head.

Ginny took the large, neatly sealed paper bag. 'Instructions are on the bottles.'

She paid her money, pocketed the change, nodded to the man with the bandaged hand, and with her eyes fixed helplessly on the face that watched her through the Vauxhall window, left the chemist's shop.

She was just walking past the window when a hand grasped her arm. A familiar voice said sharply, 'Guinevere!'

'Simon.' It was several seconds before the computer could cope with the unexpected emergency. It went mad, flinging up irrelevances, ideas, emotions, even hope, that threatened to breach the iron door.

Then the computer assumed control again. It made her repeat Simon's name with chilling disappointment, and add with apparent disarming frankness, 'Oh dear, I thought you were someone else!'

'Who?'

She slid her eyes across the road towards the Vauxhall.

'I see.' Simon didn't comment, somehow moved so that he blocked her way. 'I'm glad I ran into you.'

Ginny said nothing.

She raised her brows infuriatingly.

'I wanted to have a talk to you. I wondered why you were so odd on the phone the other evening.'

'Was I? I don't remember.'

'I do.'

'Well.' She smiled down at her feet, avoiding his eyes. 'Maybe you've got your explanation.'

She made a movement to pass him, but he didn't step aside.

'Maybe.' His mouth tightened. Then he looked down at the

package in her hands. 'You're not ill, are you?'

'No. I'm fine.'

'Who is then?'

'It's just for Eleanor. Vitamins.' She smiled brightly.

Impatiently, Shaw sounded the horn. The computer failed to suppress her quick start of anguish. 'Look, I really must dash, Simon. We're going out this evening.'

'Somewhere nice?'

'Yes?'

'Where?'

A moment's hesitation.

'John's going to decide.'

'John? John who?'

'Shaw.' She stepped backwards off the kerb. 'I must go.' She half stumbled. He put out a hand to steady her, kept hold of her arm. She felt desperate, claustrophobic with the need to escape.

'Where did you meet him?'

'Art College.' She tried to pull her arm away.

'I'll see you to the car,' Simon said smoothly.

'No, don't. He's terribly jealous.' The computer issued a self-satisfied little laugh. Registered that as a warning, Shaw had got into the driver's seat and started up the engine.

'Serious, is it, Guinevere?' Simon was propelling her across the road.

'Yes.'

Shaw watched their approach in the driving mirror.

'He's my lover,' she said, laughing, 'if that's what you mean.'

And availing herself of his start of surprise, Ginny snatched her arm free, got into the car, and immediately Shaw drove them away.


Gordon Greville lay awake listening to the small, careful

movements within the house. Not the usual sounds of an old house settling down for the night. But purposeful ones, discreet and ominous.

On the other side of the small room, his son slept with the callousness not just of youth but of his own strange nature. In these last few dreadful days since the gunmen had come, Gordon Greville's whole world had changed. The family had collapsed about him as surely as if the house had fallen down like a pack of cards. He no longer believed in them. He no longer believed in himself. He no longer believed in the ultimate decency of humanity. He no longer believed in anything. Except that none of them had much longer to live – with the possible exception of Richard. The boy might well come through.

A curious rapport between Shaw and his son seemed to have grown up. 'In his own way,' Richard had said, just before he went to sleep, 'Shaw's an idealist. He doesn't just theorize, like you lot. He does something.'

'Such as what?' Gordon had asked.

'I don't know.'

'I'm surprised they haven't taken you into their confidence.'

'Well, they haven't. I'm one of the family, aren't I?'

'Sometimes I wonder.'

Richard hadn't replied. He had simply turned over and gone to sleep. I'm no good with the boy, Gordon told himself. But then most boys of Richard's age disliked their fathers. Strike the father dead and all that. A well-known syndrome, a psychiatrist would say. But then, he doubted if he'd been much good with his daughters either. Too weak, too liberal, too permissive. Well, he wasn't weak and he wasn't liberal and he most certainly wasn't permissive any more. He had only one personal ambition left. To kill one of them before he died.

Outside, a screech owl hooted. A door opened across the landing. Rowena's room. There was a faint sound of a radio crackling and then a quick spurt of conversation, snapped off abruptly as the door shut.

Greville had turned over in his mind the possibility that the gunmen were making some kind of bomb to put aboard an aircraft. Those hessian-covered bags that he had once deluded himself into thinking carried personal belongings, more likely held lethal devices. But he could not see what point it was to hide *here* while they did so. They might, of course, have some particular airline – El Al perhaps – that they wanted to strike at, and needed to check the running of their schedule. That language of theirs was either Albanian or Arabic, he couldn't decide which. Hamid was probably an Arab, but Shaw's nationality was still a question mark. There was also the possibility that when the time was ripe the whole family were going to be used as hostages. Exchanged for certain of their comrades already in gaol. Or used to protect their getaway from a crime which had yet to be committed. And why were they so certain they would be gone by Monday? Were they listening for an aircraft that was going to collect them? Perhaps the radio was being used to listen for a signal directly to the gunmen. Perhaps they were eavesdropping on police cars and the aircraft were just incidental. Perhaps, perhaps, perhaps . . .

One certain thing was that the isolation and loneliness of the house was of paramount importance. Was its actual position also important? Why did the gunmen kill Mrs Bristowe, and yet keep the family alive? What stake was so high that they risked so much?

Just before dawn, exhausted with anxiety and unsolved questions, Gordon slipped into a brief, unsatisfying sleep. He woke with the first bird song. He got out of bed, staring out of the locked and padlocked windows at the gilding of the long brown sandbanks of morning cloud, the glow on the green stippled barks of the elm trees, the splendour of the dawn.

He longed to throw the window wide, and breathe in the cool, moist, garden-scented air. Instead, he pressed his face like a child's against the glass, drinking in the beauty, holding it to himself as a protection against whatever the day might bring. Like Mary might in her not-quite-convinced way go to church when she was acutely worried.

Once or twice in the hot days of last summer Rowena had slept out on the balcony to see the dawn, and Ginny had once, not very successfully, tried to paint it.

Over the lawn were the long shadows of oaks and elms, the black lattice-work of the balcony thrown by the rising sun.

And there in the centre, another shadow.

At first it looked like a black paper cut-out figure, holding a giant pencil. Then it was a sundial casting its pointer on the hour face. Then it was . . .

Gordon stared transfixed. Dimly he heard Richard get out of bed and shuffle over to stand beside him.

Neither of them spoke. Neither moved. They listened in complete detachment, as though all this had nothing to do with them, to the sound of an aircraft approaching Grantwick from the east. Almost directly out of the sun. The way the fighters in the last war used to come. Then they saw its little silver minnow shape. Descending lower and lower, getting larger all the time. Lowering itself confidently in the calm of an English summer morning.

And confidently, inexorably, the big black pointer on the balcony followed it down.


'What d'you make of it?'

Gordon's hand descended to his son's shoulder. Richard stood still for a few moments before shaking it free. He shrugged, pulled down the corner of his mouth. Yet there was an aura of knowing about him.

'You've a pretty good idea though?' Gordon's voice rose in key. Then with care he modulated his tone. 'Haven't you?'

'It's a rocket of sorts,' Richard said.

'A rocket?'

'That's what I said.'

'A *military* rocket?'

'Not a toy one, if that's what you mean.'

'An anti-aircraft rocket?'

'What is called a SAM. Surface to Air Missile.'

'Of what sort?'

'How the hell would I know?'

'You're the bloody expert. You're the one who knows about these things. You're the war-crazy kid. You're the one that's always got his nose in some catalogue of bloody lethal weapons.'

His son gave that strange little smile. Hateful and hating. 'And now you're glad that I did,' he said, as if the most important thing was to rub his father's nose in it.

'I'm damned well not!'

'Now I know something you don't.'

'You just said you didn't.'

'Ssh! Keep your voice down! I said I didn't know what sort.' Richard pressed his face to the window-pane. 'Could be one of several.'

'But all offensive?'

'That's an old-fashioned word. All effective. All capable of shooting down aircraft. From the right position.'

'Which we are?'

'Apparently.'

'Oh, don't be so damned off-hand about it! Apparently!' Gordon's voice had risen again. He glanced over his shoulder furtively, half expecting the gunman on the landing to burst in. 'That's what they came here for in the first place, isn't it?

It's all part of a carefully worked out plan. They've had their eye on this place for a long time. Months.' He grasped his son by the collar of his pyjamas and shook him. 'All right, all right, I know what you're going to say, so I'll damn well save you saying it. Apparently! Apparently!' He released his son, threw him to one side with a contemptuous gesture.

'So?'

'So these are the men you've sucked up to.'

'If you can't lick 'em, join 'em. Not my motto. Bill's.'

'And *admired*.'

'Perhaps.'

'And we know why.'

'Why?'

'Because there's nothing to you that makes a man so big as a gun in his hand. That's all you youngsters think about. Violence, beatings up, missiles, guns. You *need* a war!'

'There *are* wars. Here and now. It's just that we're shielded from them.'

'Thus spake thy master Shaw.'

'Don't be so damned . . .' Richard hesitated for the right word, then actually laughed. 'Offensive.'

Gordon spread his hands in a gesture of defeat. 'I give up!'

There was silence in the room. From across the intervening verdant miles of Surrey countryside came the quick puff of noise as the landed aircraft went into reverse thrust, and almost immediately the sound of another aircraft turning away from the Outer Marker down the Glide Path.

Without speaking to his father, Richard drew the curtains almost closed across the window, and then climbed up on to the deep tiled sill. He put his eye to the gap between the curtains, his head moving very slowly as he followed the aircraft and the rocket shadow with his concentrated stare.

'Well?' Gordon asked almost truculently when he climbed down.

'As I said before, I don't know exactly what sort. It could be British. Or some secret Russian job. Damn it!' he said furiously as his father's expression hardened. 'It's a shadow I'm looking at. A silhouette.'

Richard turned his back on his father, walked over to his bed and began to dress.

'All right. I'm sorry. I appreciate the difficulty. But what kind could it be?'

Irritably his son pulled yesterday's shirt over his head.

'Aren't you going to wash first?' Gordon asked in disgust.

Richard shrugged. 'Could be a Blow-pipe. Or Red-Eye. Or something like a Sam Seven.' He stepped into his jeans. 'Or it could be the Russian refinement, code name Grail.'

'Refinement!' Gordon clicked his tongue. Weightily he padded over to the washbasin and turned on the taps, every movement, every gesture trying to express a father's condemnation of his son and all his works. Richard's natural or unnatural obsession with violence. His cold, hard, ingrowing nature. His physical dirt and lack of personal hygiene.

'And what is the difference between these lethal weapons?' Gordon stripped to the waist and soaped his chest and arms.

'Not a great deal.'

Gordon sprayed himself with deodorant.

'If I might explain with this.' Richard came up behind him, took tne deodorant canister out of his hand and held it at an angle from his shoulder.

'Red-eye and Blow-pipe can be held by one man. Sam Seven might need two.'

'There are two of them up there now.'

His son shrugged. 'But the real difference is how they home. Now with Blow-pipe – ' Richard tapped the deodorant cylinder – 'the cylinder is divided into two parts. But the whole thing is entirely self-contained. The charge is in here at the top. The firing mechanism and radio tracking mechanism is here in the canister. The rocket is as simple as any round of ammunition. It can be stored. Taken out of store and fired.

Gordon stared at his son's reflection in the mirror. 'I see.' Perhaps if he stared long enough his son's reflection would vanish like Alice in the Looking Glass. Soon he would grow tall again or small. Soon he would come out of the nightmare. Normalcy would return. His beloved only son would one day return to being no more than an unlovable lout. Gangsters and criminals were for other families. Assassins and anarchists for other nations. Backward, undeveloped, uncivilized.

'There's a periscopic sight, of course. For aiming.'

Watching his son's face in the mirror, a dreadful thought came into Gordon's mind. The boy would not be averse to having a shot himself. He'd see it as little more than a game. A great outsize Colditz or shooting down enemy aircraft on Brighton Pier. A whiff from this Battle of Britain land. Tally-ho! Got him in my sights ... *putter, putter, putter.* Well done, Red three! Look out, sir, bandits at twelve o'clock high! Who were bandits and who were angels?

'Takes skill, does it?' Gordon asked.

'Some skill, yes. But in any case, it homes on the heat of the exhaust.'

'I see.'

'Some SAMs also have radar in the nose cone.'

'I wouldn't have thought it necessary.' Gordon unfolded the clean shirt that Mary had left out for him. It smelled sweet and fresh, dried out in the summer air before all this nightmare began. Raiment from another world. 'An aircraft with wheels and flaps down passing dead overhead. How can you miss?'

'The whole point is you *never* miss.'

'A bullseye every time?'

'Yes.'

'Murder?'

'Perhaps.'

'Mass murder?'

'If you like.'

'I like to call things by their proper names.'

'There is a well-thought-of theory that one murder is as reprehensible as mass murder.'

'Your friend Shaw tell you that?'

Richard smiled. 'No, you did as a matter of fact.'

'Then I was wrong.'

'So it would seem.'

'I have been obviously quite wrong in many things.' He drew on his trousers, wishing to hell that he didn't feel embarrassed at dressing in front of his son. 'But I'm not going to argue about them now. Those men have got a rocket. And they're going to fire it. Am I right?'

'Right.'

'At what?'

'Obviously a special aircraft.' He smiled as his father slowly subsided on to the end of the bed. 'And obviously an aircraft that arrives on Monday.'

Gordon's mouth opened wordlessly for a moment. Then he breathed, 'The Queen's Flight? You mean in all seriousness that they're going to shoot down the Queen's Flight?'

'Why not? Why not? Don't you see, that's what it must be.' Richard's face lit up with excitement of discovery. More quietly, he went on, 'That's the one thing that would make everyone sit up and take notice.' He paused and actually laughed. 'That *really* takes daring. That's *really* cocking a snook at the whole wide world!'

And this time, Gordon thought numbly, he wasn't quoting himself, he wasn't quoting Shaw. He was simply giving expression to his own innermost thoughts.


'Mary!' Gordon grasped her arm as she put the bread in the toaster and switched on the percolator. 'I've got to talk to you! I know what they're doing up there!'

She gave him one of her wide-eyed, distracted glances. He noticed, as it were at a distance, that her skin looked grey and crepey with fatigue.

She rounded on him reproachfully. 'You haven't even asked how Eleanor is!'

He sighed. 'How is she?'

'Oh, don't ask like that!'

'How then?'

She smiled patiently, wanly. 'Much better. She was wakeful for most of the night. I sat up with her. We talked. She needed, well, to come to terms with it, I suppose.'

Gordon nodded, wondering what difference it could make now. Certainly not to him, maybe not to them. He wondered if he should even attempt to explain himself to Mary. Explain what he must do. What if she tried to prevent him? What if her strong maternal instinct overcame her humanity? What if less likely, her love for him overcame it?

'Then,' Mary went on brightly, 'just before dawn, she drifted off to sleep. She's still flat out. Sleeping like a babe.' The ineptness of her own simile made her wince.

Gordon touched her arm. 'Just about dawn,' he said quietly, '*I* was awake.'

She looked at him, eyebrows raised, recognizing the portent of his tone. He took a step backwards and glanced through the doorway across the sitting-room to where Hamid sat behind the front door.

'The other two,' Mary said, reading his mind, 'are up in Rowena's room. Tell me quickly, before they come down.'

She busied herself with making the toast while he told her. She avoided looking at his face. Her hands continued their nervous movement; while she waited for the toast to brown, she dusted invisible crumbs off the table top, polished the gleaming toast-rack with the corner of her apron. When he came to the end, she gripped the edge of the table in both her hands, swaying on her feet, the way he'd seen on television old women sway in some devastated corner of some distant unremembered part of the world – rocking herself in anguish.

Outside the kitchen window, a robin sang. There was the cawing of rooks from the beech woods, the hum of bees, the roar of the morning flux of incoming aircraft. All underlined, timed, made finite by the furious ticking of the kitchen clock.

'So,' Gordon said gently, 'I've got to give some warning, no matter what they do to me.'

'To all of us,' Mary corrected stonily. He wanted to turn her face round to see what she meant. Was it a reminder that his first natural duty was to her, to the family?'

'To all of us,' he repeated.

She nodded.

'In a moment I shall go through into the sitting-room and ring the police.'

'Hamid will kill you.'

Gordon said nothing.

'He might even kill you before you've time to get an answer.'

'But it's worth trying.'

'Worth trying, worth trying!' She clapped her hand over her mouth to stop herself. Above her own hand, her eyes stared up at him, glazed with hysteria. Then she took a hold of herself. 'All right,' she said. 'On one condition.'

He nodded.

'I come with you.'

'Then they'll kill you, too.'

It was a stupid argument. Once the alarm was given, they would kill them all.

'With you,' she repeated.

'All right.'

She leaned over suddenly and gave him a quick girlish kiss on his cheek. She always smelled of some light flower perfume, clean and sweet. He put his arm round her shoulders and kissed her lips.

He had never felt so much that he wanted to live. He wished he could have had the last twenty years back again. He wished that all this was a bad dream. He wished that the shots from Hamid's Luger in a minute or two's time would trigger him back into wakefulness again.

Over her shoulder, he saw the second hand sweep round the face of the clock like the green arm of a radar scan. He released her gently.

'Now,' he said.

She nodded. 'Now!'

She dusted her hands on her apron and hung it behind the door. She ran a hand through her hair.

It seemed unbelievable, he thought, walking a pace ahead of her across the polished oak boards, then over the carpet, threading their way amongst the familiar pieces of their sitting-room, that this would be the place of their execution. That the telephone would be their block, the thin man by the front door their executioner.

They seemed to walk with infinite slowness in and out of the thin spotlights of sunshine that streamed through the diamond panes.

Hamid watched them with only mild alertness. Mary mimed that coffee would soon be ready. The executioner nodded, almost smiled. Then Gordon did a swift left-hand turn, stretched his arm, scooped up the telephone from the table, lifted the receiver, dialled 999.

He prayed for time for an answer before the inevitable gun fired. He noticed with a distant mournful tenderness that Mary had positioned herself between himself and the gunman.

Then nothing.

No noise. No voice. No protest. No shot. No ringing of the telephone in his hand. Just a deathly silence prolonging itself. That was it. He was dead. The alarm had been given. And in his own peculiar and unlikely way he had died a hero.

Abruptly the silence ended. The gunman shouted something. Mary turned, brows drawn together. Her expression simultaneously frightened and angry. Her eyes riveted not on him but on the telephone table.

Then he saw it – the cut wire of the telephone snaking across the polished surface of the table. He was not after all made of the stuff of heroes. He was, as Shaw had recognized, just an old fool.


'You're a fool,' Richard said, as Gordon tried to push past him. 'And you make me sick.'

I make myself sick, Gordon whispered, but not aloud. I am not a hero by nature. But neither am I by nature a murderer. Yet murder it must be. They were together in the downstairs cloakroom, the only place in the day time he could snatch a moment with his son in peace and privacy.

Outside, Mary, Ginny and Rowena were digging the trench. Eleanor was again excused, but under surveillance. She sat close by in a deck-chair between them and the gunman – the only one whom none of the family had dared to tell what the gunmen were really about.

Carefully Gordon washed his hands. 'I can't think of any other way.'

'It's just as stupid as trying to phone.'

Gordon shrugged.

'Even if,' Richard hissed, 'they hadn't cut the phone, even if you'd got through, even if the police had eventually come, it wouldn't have made any difference.'

'Yes it would.'

'No, it wouldn't! *We* – ' Richard patted his chest and then stabbed a finger beyond the cloakroom window – 'would all have got the chop.'

'I know.'

'Oh, thanks. Thank you very much, Father. Public duty and all that. The Queen's Flight must go through, what-ho-ho-ho. For Queen and Empire. Over the top, son. Up you!' He paused.

'It is five killed as against over a hundred.'

'And you were to be God!'

'I did what I thought best.'

'But, you fool, it wasn't. Just as it isn't now. If you'd given the alarm, they'd still have shot one aircraft. The aircraft are thick as flies now. They'd have taken their pick. *Any* one. Straight away before the police arrived.'

'I don't believe it.'

'Suit yourself.' Richard put his hand on the door, made as if to open it.

'Wait a moment! Help us.'

'No.'

Gordon put a hand on his arm, 'Please.'

'For the last time, no. Our only hope is to sit it out. Do what they say. Just as you said from the beginning. With any luck, they'll use us as hostages for their getaway.'

'But the aircraft? The Queen's Flight?'

Richard said nothing.

'What about Bill?' Gordon asked. 'He'll be killed too.' Richard shrugged.

'You unfeeling bastard!'

All Richard did was to smile and again shrug his shoulders. 'They might miss.'

Gordon drew in a deep breath. 'You are a monster!' he said, very slowly separating each word. 'I have bred a monster.'

Richard's smile continued to be his own individual hateful smile. 'Eugenics,' he opened the door. 'A simple matter of eugenics. Behold a monster . . . sired and damned by poisoners!'

'But what other course is open to us?' Gordon asked Mary,

when he returned to the exercise and began digging again beside her.

'None.' She shook her head. The greying hair round her temples was glued to her skin with sweat. The sunlight showed up the deep strain lines between her brows, the puckering of her lips.

'Richard won't help.'

'I didn't really expect him to.'

'If only there were some other way!' Gordon had toyed with the idea of raising their spades and making a concerted assault on the red-haired yobbo at whom Rowena kept smiling coyly. But he had his gun at the ready. The garage doors were locked. Not one of them would reach the drive, let alone run down that long exposed drive to the lane. He had thought of starting a fire. But the gunmen would put it out long before it took hold. He'd thought of trying to strangle them. But how? There was no rope. But perhaps with a pair of nylon tights? Or of stretching some trip wire across the stairs. Or of hitting them over the head. But with what? And how could he be sure that he would hit hard enough to kill?

No, poison was the only thing. Talking in urgent hurried snatches – himself to Mary and Mary to the girls, while the women dusted and cleaned, prepared food, while they dug the turning circle, always harassed by the gunman, they had taken their decision.

Though the gunmen had removed all poisons from the house, there were still the berries in the garden. In whispers, between throwing out spadefuls of earth, they made their clumsy, distasteful plan. It was Mary, the garden-lover, who had finally decided. She who had tried to raise the alarm with the flowers and failed – now again went back to the garden for help. She had hesitated between lily-of-the-valley and laburnum. But laburnum was close to where they were digging. It grew in profusion over the arch near the garage. The shrub on the south side was already well in pod. The seeds would be there. And laburnum seeds are the deadliest of them all.

Mary paused to wipe the sweat from her brow and to glance at the now diminishing cloud of pure yellow, with the greeny-yellow pods half hidden by the leaves and the un-fallen flowers. Golden Rain. *Laburnum anagyroides*. She had once used the long racemes for the Ascension Day flowers, and the vicar, complimenting her, had told her there were records of it growing in the village gardens in 1500. In some odd way it assuaged her conscience for what she was about to do.

At four-thirty, earlier than usual, Shaw appeared in the doorway and stood watching them. Measuring with his eye the progress they'd made.

'OK,' he said after a while, 'That will do. Inside.'

'But it's so early,' Mary protested.

'It is our last evening. We have much to do. And it is time you prepared supper.'

'Then please – ' Mary's voice rose – 'let me pick some flowers for the supper table.'

Shaw shrugged. 'Very well. For a few minutes – ' he smiled contemptuously – 'you may pick your flowers. But you stay in this part. Within my sight.'

Trying to disguise her haste, her nervousness, her shame, Mary stepped across the trench and broke off a couple of pink thornless roses, some stalks of nicotiana and a branch of laburnum.

'There isn't much here she can pick,' Ginny objected, drawing Shaw's eyes towards her.

'I have spoken,' Shaw replied scowling. 'There is enough.'


At six o'clock, Mary Greville took a leg of lamb and a bag of red-currant puree out of the deep freeze. It was the first time she had been able to bring herself to open the lid of the big freezer chest since the discovery of Mrs Bristowe's body there. Now the sickening remembrance of it stiffened her nerve.

She held the leg of lamb under the tap to thaw it as best she could, switched on her oven, and set about her task. She stripped the pale yellow-green pods off the laburnum twigs, her fingers eagerly seeking out every one. Then she shelled them as easily as peas. She remembered, in the inconsequential way one does remember odd remarks, that Gordon had once said that to the human mind a simple act frequently disguises a moral evil. The squeezing of a trigger, the pressing of a button that launches an intercontinental missile, the switching on of a current that electrocutes a man.

When they were all shelled, she put them in her mortar and ground them with the pestle. Then she poured them into a pan, covered them with a little water and a great mound of sugar, and cooked them until they were tender. So ordinary was her task that she had to stop herself tasting the syrup, and it was with almost a conscious effort of will that she kept the spoon from her lips. When she was satisfied with the concoction, she cooled it and mixed it with the red-currant puree and poured it into two of her best cut-glass bowls.

On the other side of the kitchen, Ginny was peeling potatoes, and slicing beans.

'Not too many,' Mary said, 'otherwise . . .'

She didn't finish. Her voice trailed. But Ginny knew what she meant. Otherwise they may not eat enough of the poison.

What are we become, Mary asked herself. Borgias, cold-bloodedly preparing a poisoned meal. How can we, as civilized people, possibly do it? Yet how can we not? We are tied hand and foot. If we shout and scream no one will hear us. We have no communication with the outside world just a mile or two away. If we marched shoulder to shoulder like the Turks did in the Korean prison, these gaolers wouldn't lay aside their arms, they would simply mow us down, and some aircraft will be exploded in mid-air.

No, the gunmen's quiet death was their only hope. They must poison them with no more compunction than if they were laying Warfarin for rats. She would like to have whispered some of her agonized thoughts to Ginny, eased her unquiet conscience, strengthened her resolve. But Ginny was tight-lipped and unapproachable. Though, at least, like Eleanor, she was on their side.

Mary couldn't decide about the two young ones. She couldn't be sure of their loyalty. It was a sign of the times, a sickness of the age. The young suborned by violent men. The Hitler Youth, the Maoists, the Palestinians, the Japanese suicide fighters, the children in Cyprus, the IRA and the UDA.

Of course, deliberately, Shaw showed a different more attractive face to Rowena and Richard than he did to the rest of them. Joked with them, showed interest in them, deferred to their opinions. Somehow, Mary was sure, he had lulled those two, if not into support, at least into neutrality. Richard had utterly set his face against the poisoning. Rowena had hesitated.

'You're just guessing,' Rowena had said when they whispered to her this morning about the Queen's Flight. 'You've not a shred of proof.'

'It was Richard's guess.'

'Well, you know him. He's a nut-case. Said it just to frighten you.'

Well, they were frightened all right, Mary thought, carefully basting the leg of lamb. And fear makes people desperate. Cruel. Murderous, even. She rubbed the browning skin of the meat with a clove of garlic. Garlic that would be hung in this same kitchen centuries ago to repel the devil. Now all that she wanted of it was to make the meal taste appetising and good.

At a quarter to seven when she could stand the silence between them no longer, she sent Ginny through to join the others in the sitting-room.

At seven, she began setting the dinner table for the gun-men's meal, and the places for the family in the kitchen. She filled a small stone jar with water and arranged the pink roses and the pale stocks and a few twigs of laburnum tolerably well. She used her linen and lace cloth with the matching napkins and her best mats. At seven-fifteen she drained the vegetables and at seven-thirty she made the gravy. A culinary time-table of murder, she thought glancing at the impassive face of the clock.

At seven-forty-five she set one bowl of poisoned jelly on the table close to Shaw's place, and another in front of the other two settings. They liked their sauces and their spices. They were good trenchermen.

At seven-fifty Gordon came into the kitchen from the sitting-room. He didn't want anything. He had come so as not to leave her alone in her guilt. A thoughtfulness in evil that moved her almost to despair.

'What are the others doing?'

'Watching television.'

'Richard too?'

'No, Richard's helping the Albanian fellow do something.'

'He wouldn't . . .?' She couldn't bring herself to say the word betray.

Gordon shook his head more firmly than he felt. 'I'll tell them to come through. That dinner's almost ready.'

At eight o'clock Mary heard the click of the lock on Rowena's door, followed by Shaw's step on the staircase. His feet crossing the sitting-room. A joke to Rowena. A forced laugh in reply. The scrape of a dining-room chair. Shaw's hands clapping for her.

'What are you serving us with this evening, Mrs Greville?'

'Your favourite. Roast lamb and red-currant sauce.'

'Excellent.' He waved to Hamid to take his place. Kuchi appeared from the cloakroom, closely followed by Richard

'Bring it in.'

Shaw looked around them all, smiling. A happy thought appeared to strike him. 'As this is our last dinner, you, Mr Greville, may eat with us tonight. Rowena, set another place for your father.'

Gordon didn't show any emotion except a mild gratification. 'Thank you.'

'You may sit while I carve.' Shaw snapped his fingers at Kuchi who handed him a knife from a sheath at his belt.

'So you really are going?' Gordon said conversationally.

'Yes. You are relieved?'

'Naturally.'

'But I said always tomorrow it would be.'

'With the apricots?' Ginny asked.

Shaw's grip on the knife tightened but he didn't answer her. 'And for tomorrow while you are all here, I tell you – ' he put the neatly carved meat on the plates and one by one handed them to Rowena who, eyes servilely lowered, put them down in front of the men – 'our arrangements.'

Shaw sat down in his place at the head of the table, unfolded his napkin and looked closely at Gordon.

'What sort of arrangements, Mr Shaw?'

'Precautions really.' Shaw seemed at pains to express himself accurately. He frowned. Absent-mindedly he spooned on to his meat a large helping of red-currant sauce. 'For instance.' He looked round the faces of the assembled family. 'It may be necessary tomorrow for some of you to stay a while in the cellar.'

Enjoying their manifest apprehension, he dipped a wad of lamb into the jelly. He raised the fork to his mouth. Mary didn't trust herself to look. Then with it half way to his lips, some involuntary indrawn breath from Rowena made him turn his head sharply.

He stared into her face. It was all written there. Guilt, terror, even pity for Shaw. His eyes narrowed as comprehension dawned. Shaw's skin paled. He licked his lips, dabbed them nervously with the napkin.

Suddenly with one of his quick cat-like movements, he leaned across the table. He snatched Gordon's plate away from him, and substituted his own.

'Eat that, old man! Eat it! Every mouthful! Go on! We are going to watch you.'

'No,' Mary shrieked. 'No, no! Don't make him! Don't, Gordon!'

'Why not?' Shaw shouted.

'Because – '

There was a whole minute's silence.

Mary hung her head. 'It was me. I put it in.'

'So!' Shaw jumped to his feet. With a furious gesture he swept the plates, and cutlery and flowers off the table and on to the carpet. 'So you are traitors, liars, cheats, whores, murderers!' He folded his arms across his chest, pale nostrils pinched, staring first at their cowed faces, and then at the mess of food on the floor and the little dobs of red jelly, eating their way into the pile of the rug.

'OK. Very well. Now you have brought your fate upon yourselves. You are enemies.' He looked slowly from Gordon to Mary to Ginny.

'But not you, Rowena. Without you, I might be dead.'

Rowena looked down at her feet but said nothing.

'Nor me,' Richard said indignantly. 'Christ almighty! I didn't have anything to do with it. I didn't know what the bloody hell they were up to. I was with Kuchi.'

Shaw nodded.

'That's certainly true,' Gordon said heavily. 'Richard was not one of us.'

'I do not require your testimony, old man. I know your son better than you do.' He exchanged a thin smile with Richard.

'Very likely,' Gordon sighed.

'We understand each other,' Richard said.

'Exactly.' Shaw's smile widened. 'Youth speaks to youth, old man. Beyond frontiers.'

'Beyond morality,' Gordon said.

'Oh, listen! Let us hear! The poisoner speaks! Morality, he says. You should be thankful I do not make you eat your own medicine.' He said something in Arabic to Kuchi, who immediately left and went upstairs two at a time. He returned almost at once carrying a coil of rope. 'But treachery must be punished. Murderers must be kept under lock and key. Is that not reasonable?'

No one answered.

'You four are guilty. You, I can never again trust. You shall be locked in the cellar. You are lucky that I let you stay alive for tonight.'

For tonight. There was a slight unintentional emphasis on those last two words, Gordon noticed. And with that emphasis went the last ray of hope. Shaw had never intended to let them stay alive. Death would come in the morning as certainly as the sun would rise.

# Locked
# on final

An atmosphere hung over Rowena's room like that of a war-time Operations Room. A feeling of expectancy, waiting, tension. The air was full of voices, though all the five occupants kept silent. On the white-painted dressing-table, sticking up above bottles of shampoo and nail varnish, phials of perfume and gold bullet tubes of lipstick was the radio, tuned in to Grantwick Tower frequency, VHF 128.1. megacycles. Throughout the night, a waterfall of voices contributed their own accented brand of English – American, German, French, Indian, Scots, Irish – asking for clearance to land.

Wearing a pair of cotton slacks and a T-shirt, Rowena sat at the dressing-table painting her nails. Richard lay on the bed. They avoided looking at each other. The french doors were flung wide open on to the balcony, on which Hamid could be seen crouched low over the range-finder. Beside him stood Shaw, with the missile up to his shoulder. Kuchi sat on a deck-chair between them, timing with a stop-watch each aircraft's descent from the Outer Marker to dead overhead.

'Clipper Three Five,' the Grantwick Controller's unhurried voice, 'Wind light and variable, visibility ten kilometres. Cloud three octas at six hundred, seven octas at fifteen hundred.'

'Roger, Tower, thank you.'

'Cleared Number One. Runway Two Six.'

'Number one . . . Runway Two Six. Clipper Three Five descending on Glide Path.'

Every run was a practice, a dress rehearsal for the Royal Flight. Every aircraft was listened for, followed to the Holding Pattern at Crowborough Beacon, checked as it came down the stack to the Outer Marker, timed immediately it reported at eighteen hundred feet, caught the moment it was visible in the prisms of the range-finder, then handed on in the eyepiece of the telescopic sight till its lights appeared in the target crosspiece, signal for Shaw lovingly to touch the trigger.

The 22.30 Air France Caravelle from Paris, the midnight British Caledonian One-Eleven from Glasgow, Pan American Clipper from Montreal, Lufthansa's one o'clock arrival from Frankfurt, a KLM charter from Tangier, a Laker Majorca package holiday return, Alitalia's night service from Rome – all reported their estimated time of arrival, all slowly descended, lights blazing through the night sky. All were monitored, timed, watched, waited for till they were vertically above the house, held momentarily in the two crossed wires of the telescopic sight – and allowed to proceed in peace and un-molested – down the Glide Path, over the green aerodrome threshold lights to a safe landing on Runway Two Six.

Everything was going like clockwork. Shaw was pleased. After the Italian DC.8 had landed, he came in from the balcony, playfully rumpled Rowena's hair, nodded approvingly at Richard, and then put his hand on the radio and began fiddling with the frequency dial.

'Can I have a go?' Richard asked, sitting up.

'What?' Shaw's attention was on the frequency band, his ears filled with the squawking cut-off voices.

'The rocket . . . can I try her?'

He might have been asking another boy for a ride on his motor bike.

'OK, Richard. OK.' Shaw smiled magnanimously. 'I have not forgotten your help. You wish to try it. Then so you shall. It is good that boys should know these things. When I was your age, already I had killed a man.'

'And it's working all right, is it?'

'Beautifully! I tell you, through the telescopic sight you can see all details perfectly. The little lighted portholes. Those yellow exhausts from the engines on which – ' he held up his finger to indicate the rocket – 'our little friend will home. Oh yes, it is a very excellent and beautiful sight! You shall see. Certainly you shall have your turn. Your crack, as they say, of the whip. Here!'

Carefully, he handed over the rocket in its canister. With enthusiasm, Richard began to examine it. It *was* British from the letters and numbers stamped on it. Two-stage booster – sustained solid propellant rocket motor.

'Proximity fuse?'

Shaw nodded. 'And on impact.'

Richard tapped the aerials on the nose cone. 'Infra-red sensors to home on the heat of the jets?'

'That is so.'

'What's this thing?' Richard had moved his hand fractionally down on to the main barrel of the rocket to a tiny brass indicator needle with a half-moon of numbers around it – 50, 100, 200, 300.

'That is only for war.'

'What *is* it, though?'

'Of no consequence. That is what they said.'

'Who are *they*?'

'That also is of no consequence.'

'Only for war,' Richard murmured. He shrugged his shoulders, touched a left-right switch on the canister. 'What about this then?'

'To steer after firing.'

'Radio-controlled?'

'That is so.'

Richard put his right eye against the periscopic sight.

'Is it not just as I said?' Shaw asked.

Richard nodded. 'Good magnification.'

'And now, Richard – ' Shaw was looking at his watch – 'it is almost two o'clock. There is a last News Bulletin, yes?'

'On Radio Two.'

'You know about these things. Would you please tune in the radio?'

'Of course.'

Richard handed back the rocket, and went into Rowena's room. He switched the radio over to the 1500 metre band. Music at first, the dying notes of a Brahms concerto. Then the six pips of the time signal on which Shaw carefully checked his watch.

Then the announcer with the last news summary.

'. . . Her Majesty's aircraft Echo Foxtrot left New York one hour ago and was last reported at longitude 65 West, flying at 38,000 feet in clear weather. It is now confidently expected that the British Airways VC10 will arrive at London Grantwick at the scheduled time of seven o'clock tomorrow morning, where the Royal party will be met by Princess Anne and her husband, the Prime Minister, Mrs Thatcher and Mr Thorpe. Security arrangements at the Airport have been stringent. Police and CID men are guarding the lounges and checking all entrances and exits. A contingent of Coldstream Guards in armoured cars are in position on the landing ramp and taxi tracks, while tanks are continuously patrolling the perimeter of the airfield. While emphasizing that nothing untoward is expected, British Airways say that after last month's terrorist outrage at Heathrow Airport, they are taking no chances . . .'

Shaw shouted out a short translation in Arabic to Kuchi. The rather puzzled expression that had been on the Albanian's face for most of the night gave way to a fat smile. '*Allahu'l aktibar!*'

'What's that mean?' Richard asked.

Shaw shook his head solemnly. 'God is the greatest!'

'Snap!' said Rowena from the bed. 'So is Mohammed Ali.'


Lying cramped on the bed beside Gordon, the ropes round her wrists and ankles chafing deep, Mary Greville had lain awake listening to the night noises of the house. She had often been wakeful like this, listening. Fallowlands creaked some nights like an old wooden ship. The floorboards, the treads on the staircase, the snuffling sound of the central heating, the queer sighs and gurgles from the ancient plumbing. And outside, the scratch of the wistaria against a window-pane, the strain of the faithless laburnum against its wires that held it to the arch, the light wind in the trees hissing like the sea. Far away, a dog fox barked, a rabbit screamed, an owl called close by. The summer night was always full of sound as a whole different world waked.

But now there were other sounds – methodical movements. Footsteps in the hall. A burst of Arabic. Faraway metallic voices from a radio. A burst of music. Half way through the night she must have dozed off. She woke to hear Rowena's voice cry out, just as she did years ago in her sleep when she was small. And then she heard Richard's step – she was sure it was his – two at a time coming down the stairs.

Where did we go wrong? Mary asked herself. They had been a normal family surely. Why, in this terrible crisis had those two separated? Was it the very young who lapped up the violence of the age? Had they the seeds of their treachery already in them? Fed on a cultural diet of violence, brought up in material affluence and moral poverty, do they simply await the coming of some violent Messiah such as Shaw? A Wonder-hero putting right the world's wrongs with a rocket?

Or was it all her fault? She had spoiled them, of course. Lavished more love on those two as her dissatisfaction with Gordon had deepened. Though they had never been well off, they lived in comfort. The younger two had never wanted for anything. Was that what it was? A mother, of course, was supposed to have special affinity with her son. So she had when Richard was small. He had been an odd little boy. Hard. Withdrawn even then. Hardly ever crying. Never moved by other people's suffering. The exact opposite of Gordon. Sometimes she used to think he made a fetish of being different from his father. Simply to annoy. Hanging old German helmets in his room, the huge poster of Che Guevara, the Japanese swords, and of recent years, the slopping around in olive-green GI surplus drabs. But the passion for guns and war was real enough. She used to laugh at Gordon's anger. 'At least we know what to buy him for birthdays and Christmas.' Models of warplanes and tanks and rockets cluttered his tables, hung on strings from the ceiling. The floor was littered with valves and wires from the inside of radios. She could always rely on getting rid of him for days with a packed lunch at Farnborough Air Show and Biggin Hill. But all that was natural, surely. Boys were like that. Gordon, if he hadn't been, was the exception that proved the rule. It was a fantasy phase. Not like Rowena's – clumsily, hungrily waiting for her first romance. Casting even an assassin like Shaw for a dashing romantic role. But a fantasy of violence, power, the ability to kill your enemies? No, it was more than that. Her thoughts came full circle. There was within Richard some Stygian darkness. She had glimpsed it in his attitude to them all. The grudging way he did even the smallest job for her.

The sneering tone he used to his father, his beastliness to his sisters. Even his attitude to himself. Scruffy, long-haired, unclean.

'If you ever were in your precious army,' Gordon had once shouted at him, 'you'd have to smarten up. Get your hair cut.'

And, prophetic words, Richard had yelled back, 'The army I get in won't gripe about trifles.' Prophetic words indeed. He had been recruited now into some army of world-wide anarchy.

Who would have thought a week ago that this could have happened? In the soft south-east of safe secure England? Who would have thought that the family would be thus divided, and the younger two gone over to the enemy? Collaborators, no less.

Maybe Gordon was right and that subconsciously old men bring about wars to kill off the young. Because the young are full of power and violence. Unstable. A menace to their society. Natural forces, volcanoes, waiting to erupt and destroy and change the landscape of the world.

Mary closed her eyes tight shut as if to clamp off the terrifying pictures that flowed through her brain. It was no use, she thought, turning her head from side to side. However much she might try to blame Richard or Rowena or Gordon, basically it was her fault. She had indulged the younger two. And in some curious unspoken way, she had shown them she despised Gordon. Perhaps she had shown the gunmen that, too.

It was symbolic that it was she who had been impressed in the first place by Shaw, by his salesman's patter. She who had invited him into the house. She who had ordered the photograph. She who had let Shaw inspect the house minutely, take her measure, size up the family situation and move in. She had brought murder and death to this house.

She had failed to save Mrs Bristowe. She had failed to

save Eleanor's baby. And when she was allowed out into the village to do the church flowers, she had failed to give warning. Even the poison attempt was a failure.

Now because of her, how many more would lie entombed in the cement of the turning circle? How many more, after the Queen's aircraft exploded, would lie dead and mutilated over this English countryside? And what a chain reaction of calamities would follow such a blow to the whole nation!

Even her prayers, such as they were, had failed. No miracle had been forthcoming. No one had interpreted the message of the flowers. Now a miracle would be required of such magnitude that it would be beyond the range of that aloof glass shepherd in the east window. She remembered sadly how years ago, Ginny and Eleanor used to go to a small convent school when they lived on the other side of Medbridge.

A fête was held every year in June. The small children ran races. Parents baked cakes and scones, organized teas on the lawn, hoopla and white elephant stalls, and buried treasure. Always there was apprehension amongst the parents lest it rained.

Then, nearly always on the day, looking back, it seemed, the sun had shone. She remembered the nuns walking about in their long black habits, nodding their white starched coifs, smiling. Surprised at the parents' relief at the fine weather. 'But we prayed and the dear Lord answered.'

Mary had marvelled that their faith should be nourished by so very little. Felt a mixture of warmth and pity for their naivety. She remembered standing in the convent doorway, smiling inwardly, the one time a rainstorm had burst just as the last stall had been cleared away. Six o'clock. She could still see Mother Aloysius striding in with the last roll of bunting under her arm, her beaming face upturned to the heavy sky, great drops of rain falling on her starched coif, making a noise like rain on summer leaves.

'We prayed, and the dear Lord held the rain till the right time!'

Another miracle. Mary had laughed afterwards to Gordon. The dear Lord couldn't lose. Nor could He help them now, Mary thought bitterly. The dear Lord, the rain and sun-maker, had no sufficiently large miracle that he could per-form. Except perhaps to ease her feeling of intolerable guilt.

For all these last hours that they had been down the cellar, she had tried to pray. It was all that remained. But she felt that she had somehow placed herself beyond this by all her failures and by her attempt to kill the gunmen. Now she repeated, in silence, the words of the general confession. The only prayer, she had once told Eleanor, of the whole service which she could say with conviction. Then other prayers that she remembered from childhood, from her irregular, half hopeful, half disbelieving churchgoing, from Eleanor's wed-ding, and one from her own. The repetition calmed her nerves, quietened her heartbeat. She thought more quietly about the family. She wondered if Ginny would have married Simon, if they lived through all this, or if all this had never happened.

After a while she twisted herself round, moved her bound hands, felt the worn stuff of Gordon's old sports jacket, and clumsily moved down his arm till she found his hands. They were limp with sleep, but she managed to twine her own gently through them.

Uncomfortable as she was, she must have dozed off. She woke to a sound. Soft at first, no more than a whisper. Then getting gradually louder. Settling to a steady thrumming sound. Rain. Rain rattling on the barred window. Rain splashing on the summer leaves.

She had prayed, Mary thought. She had managed to pray. And the dear Lord, her frail glass shepherd, had not managed to send deliverance, not even fête-day sunshine. All he had managed to send was rain.

Leaning against the rails of the balcony, Richard felt a cold wet sting on the back of his hand. He was rubbing it against the thick wool of his sweater when another sting, bigger and wetter, pricked his forehead, trickled down his cheek.

He looked up. Two miles due west a small brooch of ruby, diamond and emerald lights glistened against a black velvet setting – the Lufthansa 707 from Frankfurt turning on to the runway heading over the Outer Marker.

No one else on the balcony had felt or seen anything. Shaw had his right eye pressed hard against the rocket microscopic sight. Hamid was bent over the range-finder. Kuchi was on watch from the landing window. Rowena still lay on the bed, eyes closed now, apparently asleep.

'Hamid . . . see him yet?'

'No, but I hear his engines.'

Two more drops in rapid succession, then five, six, seven running into his eyes, the jewelled brooch became blurred, then vanished into the pocket of the night. Shaw called out again – this time something about focus.

The next moment, the roof of the sky caved in. Water streamed down on top of them. Above the rattle of the rain could be heard the thunder of jet engines dead overhead, but not a sign of the 707 could be seen.

'What is this?' Shaw yelled at Richard.

Richard shrugged his shoulders. 'Rain.'

'But how much?' Shaw took the rocket off his shoulder put it down on the balcony floor, and stared anxiously up into the overcast. 'How long, Richard?'

But there was no answer. Richard had already made for the shelter of Rowena's bedroom. Angrily Shaw followed him inside, with Hamid trotting obediently behind him like a damp shadow carrying the range-finder. 'Is not forecast!'

'Actually, they did say something about showers.'

'This . . . shower!' Shaw shouted. 'Is *storm*!'

Rowena opened her eyes. 'What's the matter now?'

'Only seconds ago . . . stars!' Shaw snatched at the tuning knob of the radio on the dressing-table, turned off the Tower Controller, and switched on the continuous meteorological service on 126 mcs. '. . . temperature 18, dew point 15, cloud five octas at 2000 . . . visibility ten kilometres . . .'

The weather in Manchester.

'Your forecaster!' Shaw's face was flushed. 'Always wrong!'

'It never stops raining here,' said Rowena. 'You get used to it.'

Attracted by the shouting, in came Kuchi from the landing through the open door. He said something in Arabic, clearly about the weather and the fact that he couldn't see anything either, collecting a furious retort from Shaw.

'Is not right!' Shaw put both his hands in his pockets and walked over to the window. 'Look!'

The balcony was already a small square lake, pock-marked by the continuous raindrops. In the centre, like a small volcanic island, stood the rocket in its canister.

'*Petit pauvre!*' said Rowena.

'I am not poor!'

'Keep your hair on! It's Sam I mean.'

Her remark alerted Shaw to the plight of the missile. He barked something at Kuchi who went outside, took off his coat, draped it round the rocket's steel shoulders and returned to Shaw's ranting.

'What's the worry?' Richard added. 'Even if you don't see the VC10, you can fire blind by the time from the Outer Marker.'

'The wind may change. They may use the other runway.'

'There *is* no wind.'

'But there is rain!'

'So what?'

'They may divert!' Shaw screamed at him. 'They may go to Heathrow.'

'Weather will be the same there.'

'Or Hurn or Manchester or Prestwick!'

'What, with all the Reception Committee waiting?'

But Shaw would not be calmed. 'A royal personage . . . they would not dare.'

'The pilot will land blind on the ILS.'

'Even so.'

'And it'll probably clear up just as suddenly as it came on.'

'It's worse!' Shaw said. 'Look at it now!'

Out on the balcony it was one continuous curtain of rain. Kuchi's coat, heavy with water, had slipped off the shoulders of the rocket down on to the canister. Plagued perhaps with ideas of rust getting in the delicate working, water shorting circuits, damp extinguishing the power of the explosive, Shaw yelled Arabic at Kuchi, who, perspiring, went out again into the rain.

He collected the missile and his coat in his huge arms and began waddling back into the bedroom.

'Careful!' Shaw shouted at him.

Unceremoniously, he deposited his burden on the foot of the bed, just below Rowena's drawn up legs.

'*Do* you mind?'

Kuchi wiped the sweat and the rain off his small brow.

Rowena wrinkled up her face fastidiously. 'Take the thing away!'

Shaw said, 'Very wet. Better dry it.'

Kuchi leaned forward and began pulling his coat off the missile canister. There was a sudden rattle and tinkle.

'What the hell's that?' Shaw demanded.

'Something's fallen out of his top pocket,' Richard said.

'What?'

'Pen . . . no, screwdriver . . .'

'Where is it now?'

'Inside the canister. Slipped between the fin flanges.'

'*Quel dommage,*' said Rowena.

'Get it out.' Shaw gave Kuchi a punch and a kick. '*Get it out!*'

A fat fist unfolded and tried to squeeze itself between the curve of the canister metal and the rocket.

'Better take the missile out of the canister,' Richard said.

'I will not! *I will not!*' Shaw shouted. 'We will never get it back. They said . . . do not touch. Just fire.'

'I can get it back.'

'There is no time.'

'There's *loads* of time.'

'We won't take the rocket from the canister.'

'May have to. Only way of getting the thing out.'

Kuchi was standing on one foot, looking sheepish. Shaw glared at his watch and winced. He pulled Kuchi's hands away from the missile, and tried to insert his own fingers. When these clearly were too large, he looked at Rowena, pulled her up off the pillow, grabbed her hand and stretched the small fingers out straight.

'*Pardonnez-moi, monsieur.*'

'Go on!' he told her. 'You try!'

Obediently, the fingers gingerly descended down the metal gap.

'Feel anything?'

She nodded. '*Quelque chose.*'

'Pull it out.'

'*Ce n'est pas possible.*'

'Do as I tell you!'

He had got hold of her by the nape of her neck as though he were a puppet that he was manipulating. As she tried to wriggle away, his grip hardened.

'It's too slippery.'

'Get it between your forefinger and your thumb.'

'Too far down.' She was withdrawing her hand when he grabbed her wrist and started pushing it down the side of the launching canister again.

'Here . . . you're *hurting*!'

'Get it! You can . . . you can! And hurry!'

She was touching it now. The thing began making a rattling noise.

'There . . . that's it.' Shaw began stroking the back of her neck. 'Now grip it between your fingers.'

'I'm trying to.'

'Then pull up.'

Infinitely slowly, Rowena began edging her hand upwards.

'You're doing it!'

The knuckles appeared, then joints in her fingers, then a small pocket screwdriver caught like a thin silver eel between the bright red nails.

'Good girl!' Shaw gave an explosive sigh of relief, then turned on to Kuchi a long spiel of angry Arabic. The big man seemed to crumple, grow smaller under the furious tirade.

'Go on then!' At last Shaw relapsed into English. 'Get us breakfast. It is all you are good for. And you – ' he called over his shoulder to Rowena – 'you go with him! Otherwise he will make a mess of that too.'

Rowena rose from the bed and stretched herself. 'What do you want?'

'Tea . . . sandwiches . . .'

'And . . . the others?'

'What do you mean?'

'The four in the cellar.'

Shaw considered the matter. 'All right. But they are not to be untied.'

He pushed Kuchi and the girl towards the open door throwing a last warning to Rowena in English, 'And he will watch you, miss! So no funny business!'

'*Quel drôle!*'

The door closed behind the two of them. Silence descended, broken only by the rattle of the rain on the glass of the french doors and the monotonous meteorological clatter on the radio. Grantwick was giving simply showers, and Hamid had tuned back to 110 mcs, the Approach frequency.

'Is strange girl, your sister . . . but willing.'

'Which one?'

'*That* one.' Shaw jerked his head towards the doorway as though Rowena still stood there. 'The other – ' he did not trouble to include Eleanor – 'is she-devil, no woman.'

'Ginny's not so bad when you get to know her.'

'Know her? Do I not *know* her!' With difficulty, Shaw managed to change the contortions of his face into a crooked smile. 'But you, Richard, you're different.'

'Bastard, that's me,' Richard said equably.

'No, no . . . you very good boy. You understand. You *sympathique*. You are clever too. Very clever. Not like Kuchi . . . big clumsy dummkopf. Not like Hamid.' He took no notice of the fact that Hamid stood beside him, wiping the last drops of moisture off the gleaming cone of the missile with his handkerchief. 'Just peasant, really. Knows nothing. Me – ' he pointed at himself – 'I am clever, very clever. But you have education, technical education . . . mechanics, radio. I . . . I have other things.' He put his arm over Richard's shoulders. 'Go far . . . the two of us. You and I . . . brothers. Go very far.'

Shaw's mood had quietened. He actually smiled. 'Am sorry I was angry.'

'Anyway – ' Richard pointed to the window – 'rain's slackening.'

'I saw.'

'Just a shower.'

'I know . . . I know. But I feared it would get worse. The

VC10 would go elsewhere. All would be lost.' Shaw shrugged his shoulders deprecatingly. 'Are very worrying, these . . . affairs.'

'You've done this sort of thing before then?'

Shaw nodded.

'How many times?'

A secretive look came over Shaw's face. 'Once, twice, maybe more.' He jerked his head at the SAM still lying on the flowered quilt. 'But never such a big operation.' He waved his arms in a wide impressive gesture. 'Never so ambitious. Never so much trust – ' he touched his chest and bowed his head – 'put in these humble hands.'

In the background, the Grantwick Controller was talking to an Air France Caravelle that seconds later came whistling overhead. Hamid peered out, nodded and pointed to where the twin cones of the landing lights pierced the drizzling half-darkness.

'There was no need to worry.'

'This I see. Everything will be all right now. I have said to you I am sorry. I am sincere man. I am sorry for many things. Yes, you smile, Richard, but I am sorry. Sorry that lives must be lost.' He waved at the rocket. 'But I do not kill in malice.'

'That makes it OK?'

Shaw was not sure if it was a question or a statement, but he nodded. 'Of course. Your Queen has not personally harmed me. Just as – ' he stabbed a finger at Richard – 'she has not personally helped you. But she is a symbol. For you. So for me.' He smiled reminiscently. 'When we train a little for this . . .'

'Where do you do that?' Richard asked eagerly.

Shaw shrugged. 'Here and there. It is not important. When we train for personal killing . . .'

'You mean hand to hand combat?'

Shaw nodded. 'We have on the stuffed dummies a face.

Nice! Our enemy. He can be who you wish. It gives great effect.'

'They do that in Japan,' Richard said. 'They call it boss-bashing.'

'Good, good! They are very clever people, the Japanese. Make good fighters. Freedom fighters.'

'Who do you put on your dummy?' Richard asked. 'A Jew?'

'Perhaps. Perhaps,' he laughed playfully, 'a fox-hunting Englishman.'

'My father isn't exactly that.'

Shaw shrugged. 'He is nothing.'

Richard didn't deny it. 'What about the family, though?' he asked, as if he'd just been reminded of it.

'I am sorry about the cellar. But after last night!' Shaw scowled. 'That was very wicked. I was shocked to the heart.' He touched his breast. 'After a guest has eaten salt, it is great evil . . .' He sighed. 'Death would be – '

'You weren't exactly welcome guests,' Richard interrupted.

Shaw burst out into excited laugher. 'No, I tease you. They will be released.'

'Unharmed?'

'*Ayoa* . . . you know what that means?'

'Yes.'

'Yes . .' Shaw mimicked him. '*La illsha il i'Allah.*'

'There is only one God.'

'You are learning, you see! Why trouble yourself with people who are dead anyway? You are of the new world. You are young. You are a rebuilder.'

'Destroy first. Then rebuild?'

'Exactly.'

'And when d'you release them?'

'Ah,' Shaw smiled. 'You want to know the plan.'

'It would help.'

'And you will help us?'

'If you like.'

'I do like. And if I like what you do . . . very good that, eh? If I like what you do, they,' he pointed down, 'will be all the sooner free. Happy, what you say? Free as air. Now – '

Shaw sat on the edge of Rowena's bed, at a careful distance from the rocket. He looked at his watch. 'We have ninety minutes before Echo Foxtrot arrives. Yes?'

'Check. Ninety minutes.'

'Soon we shall eat breakfast. Then we shall tidy, leave everything in order. After work, clear decks for action. Right?'

'Right.'

'Now when action is complete – '

'The aircraft destroyed?'

'Yes.' Shaw nodded. 'There is need for great haste.'

'The authorities will assume a bomb on board.'

'Nevertheless, we must move fast. So as soon as Echo Foxtrot is cleared to the Outer Marker, Kuchi will go down and start the Land-Rover's engines. Hamid will man the range-finder. You will have the stop-watch and tune the radio. I will fire. Then we will take all down to the Land-Rover and go.'

'We?'

'Hamid, Kuchi, Rowena, you, me.'

Richard nodded.

'As soon as we are safely on the boat, your sister may go. She shall have the key to the cellar. She may release your family, but will say nothing.'

'And . . . me?'

'You will want to come with us. This I know.'

'As a hostage?'

'No, Richard, no. Of course not. That is a silly word.'

'But it's what we're really doing up here now, isn't it? You're keeping us close to grab us if anything goes wrong.'

'You are so wrong.' Shaw put his hand on Richard's shoulder and pressed it weightily. His tone was emotional. 'You are my friend. I am very sincere. I like you. You will leave your family, your society . . . and join ours.'

Richard nodded, smiled as though reassured. 'I see now.'

'You agree?'

'*Ayoa.*'

'Richard.' Shaw smiled broadly. 'You speak my language!'


Twenty feet above Gordon Greville's head, the door was flung open. A waterfall of electric light from the back lobby streamed down the cellar steps. Framed in the lintel, was Rowena holding a tray. And immediately behind her, the big black silhouette of Kuchi.

'Breakfast.' His youngest daughter's voice echoed round the stone vaults. Like a soprano trying a note above her range. Attempting gaiety, reaching shrill. But blithely enough, it seemed to Gordon, as she tripped down the stone steps to the uneven floor. She wore one of Mary's aprons round her neat waist. She might have been a maid bringing in the morning tea in some strange hotel. A total stranger.

Like a maid she paused by their grilled window. The sunlight flung the shadow of her head behind the little bars on the floor. 'Nice day,' she said, talking determinedly against the silence. 'Sun's coming out.'

Nobody spoke. Ginny turned her head away. Beside him, he could see Mary watching Rowena steadily, her expression deepening into one of puzzled dismay. Did thus, he wondered sadly, some German mother look at the Hitler Youth, some parent at an IRA terrorist? He suddenly remembered the mother and father of the Kray brothers being interviewed on television and their protesting that their sons were such nice lads, loving children, doting on animals, loyal to the Queen. Perhaps all parents see like that. Never knowing the dark side of their offspring. Seeing their bright moon faces just as reflections of their own unalterable sun. Till some day, dark spoke to dark and they were away.

Eleanor smiled, but uncomprehendingly, as though far away.

'Coffee. And sandwiches. Sorry they're only marmalade. But it was all I could find.'

Inches behind her, a black shadow, Kuchi moved in step with her every movement.

'Can't untie you, I'm afraid. Orders.' She stooped over her father. 'But there's a couple of straws, and if I put the cup here on the floor you can reach. And the sandwich. Do eat . . .'

Her head was very low, right over his, her big blue wide-open eyes above him did not now reflect the half inane, half frightened gaiety of her voice. Nor was there mesmerized obedience, nor calf-love sickness, nor despair, nor indifference. There was entreaty.

'Difficult, I know. But eat. I'll put your sandwich on the pillow beside you.'

'Mother . . .'

There was no sound from Mary.

'I'll arrange yours the same. There.'

She walked to the other side of the cellar.

'Eleanor. Here's yours.'

Eleanor immediately and thirstily reached her head down.

The sound of sucking mixed with the brisk clicking of Rowena's heels.

'Now Ginny – '

Somehow Ginny managed to raise her shoulders off the bed, stick out her elbow, and strike Rowena hard in her stomach. There was the clatter of the tin tray, the slap of spilled coffee, the rattle of the paper cups.

'Ginny, you bitch!' Rowena exclaimed in her normal voice.

Kuchi stepped forward, raised his arm and gave Ginny a slap across her face that sent her bouncing back on the mattress. The bedstead rattled.

Then he took Rowena roughly by the shoulder, and began bundling her back up the steps. The door banged shut. The key turned. Silence again.

From the high-up little window, as though from a film projector, a shaft of sun slanted a picture of five iron bars on the stone screen of the floor. Dust particles danced up and down in it. Dust to dust. Inexorably as a sundial, the picture slid slowly to the right

When will it be, Gordon Greville asked himself. When will they come for us? They had taken away his watch. He had no idea of the time, except that it must be an hour or so after dawn.

Not very long now and the Queen's VC10 would arrive over Grantwick. Not long now and the pilot would be reporting at the Outer Marker. Not long now and he would be beginning his slow vulnerable descent to dead overhead . . .

Outside a whole chorus of birds sang and called. Then beyond and above it, faintly and faraway, the sound of an aircraft. Was this the one?

All four of them were listening. Gradually the sound became louder, the whistling high, higher, higher still. During the war, on his firewatching duties, Gordon had prided himself on being able to recognize an aircraft by the sound of its engines – the song of the Spitfire, the boom of the Lancasters, the buzz of Fortresses, the de-synchronized discordance of a Heinkel III. But now it was different, or his older ears less finely tuned. All jets sounded alike. A hard piping, like steam escaping from the safety valve of a huge pent-up cylinder.

*Whoosh* – a roaring and a rushing sound dead overhead. Then gradually dying away into a sigh from a collapsing balloon.

Not that one.

'Gordon, your coffee will be cold.'

Mary might have been calling him back to the vanishing past. To a living, working day beginning. Instead it was . . .

what day? The day of death and calamity? The day that would go down in all the history books? The day the Queen and the Royal Party and all the souls on board her aircraft were assassinated? The day the whole Greville family were wiped from the face of the earth?

Not quite. Rowena and Richard had earned their safe-conduct. And how did one view that aspect? With thankfulness? With gratitude for that mercy? Would one want them to share the same fate? And yet would one want . . . the other?

He wondered whether the others had come to some conclusion about their probable eventual fate. He hoped not.

He had himself decided that there was only one possible course for the Arabs to follow. The four of them would be killed so as to eradicate all possible chance of raising the alarm and identification after the deed had been done, in much the same way as Mrs Bristowe had been eliminated. After all, they had served their purpose during the last five days. They had been available on tap to answer the telephone and eradicate all possible suspicions. Rowena and Richard would be kept as hostages for the escape.

The sound of another aircraft now. Lower and louder. This would be the Queen's VC10.

There was a dead silence in the cellar as they all listened.

The engines reverberated in a clatter of uneven noise. The undercarriage would be coming down now, he had seen and heard the same thing so often before. Now more regular as the pilot settled on the Glide Path of the Instrument Landing System – all the time getting louder.

The whistling reached a crescendo. Just over the house, that *whooshing* noise again.

Silence again.

Not that one either.

But the aircraft were all coming right over the house. At five hundred feet range, a huge target with a span of a hundred and sixty feet, how could Shaw possibly miss?

The bright rectangle of molten sunshine crossed with the five bars had moved six feet across the cellar floor. Outside he heard two jays quarrelling, the cawing of rooks, the roo-coo-coo of wood pigeons.

'Gordon, eat something.'

He turned his head on the pillow and saw his wife's eyes looking at him. The same deep blue as Rowena's. The same expression, too, urgent and pleading, as had been on his youngest daughter's face. Strange that flesh and blood should be the same and yet so different. To please Mary, he moved his shoulders, twisted round and began to eat the clumsy sandwich.

Rowena had never been much good in the house. Chunks of bread, thick butter, huge dobs of marmalade. It ran down his chin. Disgustedly, he almost gave up. Then his tongue grazed against a sharp edge. His teeth bit into something hard. Squinting down into the crumbling folds of the sandwich, he saw the glint of silver.


'Allah is good!'

Shaw smiled, hands spread wide in his typical extravagant gesture of delight, as the British Caledonian aircraft, reporting over the Outer Marker, disclosed itself in Hamid's range-finder as a VC10. Allah in his infinite wisdom and in his manifest support had sent him for his dress rehearsal the identical aircraft as the one for the Royal Flight. 'It is a sign,' he went on, a grateful gaiety tinging his voice. He turned up his face to the fragments of blue in the clouded sky. 'Also the weather. No more rain!'

From the doorway of Rowena's room, Richard said, 'What did I tell you?'

'Silence, please!' Shaw raised his hand. 'You may come and watch. But keep quiet! Tell your sister also.' He frowned over his shoulder through the glass at Rowena. 'Silence! We are, as you say, operational. This must be exactly as for Rea Flight.'

He glanced at Hamid carefully following throu.... ...ne range-finder the progress of the little silver minnow as it swam silently in and out of cloud rocks and caverns. Then Shaw drew in a deep breath, flexed his fingers, and with a strange exalted look, raised the rocket to his shoulder.

No one on the balcony spoke. Hardly breathing, it seemed, the three of them watched the fish swell, disclose its distinctive tail, become a glittering gondola smoothly travelling the lower canals of the air. But caught nevertheless in the crossed wires, black-edged like an in memoriam notice. Dead already, if they so chose. Neither a fish nor a gondola nor an aircraft. Just a butterfly taken out of the killing bottle and pinned in a glass case.

'Allah is good!' Shaw repeated.

Below them, the drenched garden shimmered in the intermittent shafts of morning sun. There were cobwebs on the shrubs and hedges spangled with dew. The lawns shone with the blue bloom of sodden grass. And beyond the hedges, the fields steamed. White morning mist still clung in the woods like fleece caught in a sheep fence. Behind them in Rowena's room, like the fourth member of the team, came the Grantwick Controller's voice and the little black pinned shape answering him.

'Caledonia Six Five Nine . . . on Glide Path at fifteen hundred descending.'

'Roger, Six Five Nine. Wind calm, QNH 1019. Cloud six octas at seven hundred feet, visibility four kilometres.'

'Roger, thank you.' Oblivious of the black crossed eye that followed him, the pilot's voice replied. Slow unhurried English. Fair weather, piece of cake.

'Runway Two Six.'

'Any other traffic?'

'Nil.'

Now he was within range. Now Shaw put his eye to the microscopic sight. 'Now I have him,' he said.

Drawn by his excitement, Rowena came over and stood beside the door.

'Six Five Nine is visual.'

Now he was turning. Banking slightly on one long tapered wing, big now, showing his formidable vulnerable size. A mammoth, a whale, an unarmed creature of the prehistoric past, not built to withstand the assaults of this new crueler age of terror.

'Six Five Nine coming up the Middle Marker.'

Nose towards them now, tamely as if they were playing him on a long thin line – down, unstruggling, he came. Making a great whale-like bellowing of useless sound, showing like some foolish tickled trout the soft thin skin of his throat. Then the scream as the flaps descended, the visible hesitation.

'Six Five Nine is cleared, Number One.'

'Allah is good, yes!' The three great oleo legs and the undercarriage that must look in the eyepiece as if they were going to touch Shaw's head. Sweetly and obligingly, the VC10 slowed. 'I see all so clear! So beautifully clear!'

Then the aircraft was sweeping directly over them for the winking of an eye, blotting out the early morning sun.

With infinite measured gentleness, Shaw's finger lightly touched the release trigger. Then the sun shone again, and in a scream of sound the aircraft was gone.

For a moment Shaw stood absolutely still with the SAM pointing directly upwards, visibly moved. It was as if he had been through some mystical experience, as though he had briefly known what it was like to be God.

'I had him,' he said, addressing his remark to the Controller's voice now busy with after landing instructions.

Slowly, lovingly, Shaw lowered the rocket, his eye still

at the sight, seeing the drifts of clouds magnified and made even more beautiful by the telescopic lens. It was as if, lover-like, he could not bear to let the beautiful experience he had just had go. A smile touched his lips. He lowered the missile to the tree-tops.

'I can see black untidy birds,' he said.

'Rooks.'

'Not nice.' He pretended to pull the trigger, and laughed. He lowered the rocket gently, reverently, down almost to horizontal.

Then his whole body froze, the smile vanished, his expression darkened.

'I see – ' his voice sank to a hissing whisper – 'a man.'

'Can't,' Richard said.

'I see a man!' Shaw's voice shook with anger. 'Look for yourself! It is that man of Guinevere's!'

Visibly controlling his anger, cautiously he handed the missile to Richard. The boy put the sight up to his eye. A tall figure was just emerging from the misty wood, hands in his pockets, head down, not looking in their direction. Richard felt his throat tighten, but with what emotion he couldn't analyse.

'Who is it?' Rowena asked.

'Simon.'

'But what is he doing?' Shaw asked.

'How the hell would I know?' Richard said.

'But, Kuchi!' Shaw demanded of Hamid. 'Why did he not see him?'

Followed by the other Arab, he began striding into the bedroom, shouting through the open door down the landing. 'He is the one that is watching the lane!'

'Simon's taken a short cut through the woods, that's all,' Richard called after them.

'But why?'

'Probably stopping up the fox earths.'

'Yes?' Shaw looked doubtfully from Richard to his sister. 'But he has field-glasses.'

'Simon always carries field-glasses,' Richard said. 'Anyway, he's half a mile away. He's not coming here.'

Shaw still frowned. Still followed by Hamid, he walked angrily through Rowena's room to the door to the landing. Over his shoulder, he said to Richard, who held the rocket to his shoulder, 'Put that down. Carefully! *Carefully, now!*'

'No need to panic.' Richard still kept the missile up as though obsessed, while the nose cone turned polished silver in the glint of the sun. 'Simon's gone away.'

'He did not stay long,' Shaw said, reverting to his exalted mood. 'Just to give for me here – ' he touched his chest – 'a fright.'

'For me too, he stayed – ' Richard gentled his fingers down the missile – 'just long enough.'


Those words echoed in Rowena's head. False, delusory. Richard was after all Richard. She must be untormented by hope. She caught a glimpse of her brother's absorbed profile as he delicately, lovingly ran his hands from the pointed cone down the smooth sides of the rocket. Had not there been an opportunity? With both Arabs' attention distracted away from the rocket, could not Richard have altered something? After all, he was genned up on these things. But as soon as she thought that, she recognized it was useless. She'd picked up enough technical information these last few days to know that from the position of the balcony, with the aircraft at that height, slowed by its flaps, the gunmen couldn't miss.

Besides, there was the steering mechanism with which Shaw could visually correct the rocket's course. And last and deadliest of all, there was the heat of the engines, which would pull the rocket on to the aircraft like a magnet.

There was no hope. There was nothing that any of them

could do. Nothing Richard could do, even if he were so disposed. The gunmen's plan had been too well prepared. Luck had been on their side. The clockwork precision of the Royal programme. The now fine weather. The fact that, as usual, every bit of the vast Security network was concentrated on the airfield. The incoming influx of aircraft had already ceased in anticipation of their arrival.

Rowena clasped her hands and stared down at them blankly. Her mind was like the radio. Its emptiness scratched by the random static of unsupported hopes. So little luck had been on their side. If only last night's cloudburst had swollen to a violent continuous storm. If only it had made them divert the Royal Flight. If only it had caused something more dramatic than Kuchi losing his screwdriver, which she did not know if her father would find, and God alone knew how he could use, even if he did.

Shaw looked at his watch, gestured to Hamid to take up his position on the range-finder. 'It is already almost seven,' he announced. 'We must all be at readiness!'

Everything seemed loud now against the silence in the room. But removed and unreal. Bird song. The scuffling of thrushes among the flower-bed leaves. The odd distant car along the lane. At Rowena's school, they still observed the two minutes' silence on November 11th, Remembrance Day. The whole assembled school waiting with bowed heads in breathy uncomfortable silence for the gun salute to go off, the mournful time to end and life to begin again. It was like that now, except that appalling death would end it – not life.

'Soon . . . they arrive!' Shaw clasped his hands. He glanced over his shoulder at the silent radio. He looked from Hamid to Richard. 'Nothing wrong with that, is there?'

Richard shook his head. 'Still on Grantwick Approach.'

'*You* haven't touched it?'

Shaw stood in the doorway and addressed a nervous

Rowena. His voice was accusative, his dark eyes bright with suspicion. Handsome, attractive. Evil. She could still not bear to look at him without a catch of misery. A mixed self-destroying misery. She was, she knew, not beautiful like Ginny. She had no charm. Nor had she Ginny's strange charisma of bitter-sweetness. She was clever at school, yes. But she was seventeen and a half, and academic success was no longer enough. She wanted men to be attracted to her. From the beginning, she recognized it now, she had built up her weird romantic dream of the man in the wood. She had trodden down a nest into which Shaw, the murderer, had stepped as a hero. And even without her adolescent preparation, he had his own sinister magnetism. He had set out to attract her, to make her believe, to convert her to faith in him and his glib principles.

Rowena remembered, two years ago, being given a reefer which her next-door neighbour on the school bus had urged her to try. Ever game for a scientific experiment, Rowena had smoked it. She was promised that the reefer would stilt her up, sharpen her already artistic perceptions so that she saw every leaf and flower, every cloud and every blade of grass, in hitherto unrevealed beauty and colour.

Instead, the effect had been distortion. Horizons had blurred, buildings lost their definition. Every decision seemed too heavy to take. She couldn't remember which foot she set off with. She couldn't judge the depth of the steps down from the bus. And though she had known all along that she would soon come out of this unnatural state of being, while it lasted it was wholly real.

Shaw's first effect had been similar. Her instinct had told her he was evil. But his arguments, his personality, his animal attraction were powerfully persuasive.

Rowena folded her arms over her chest. There were still the prints of Shaw's fingers on her skin where he had man-handled her when she tried to phone. Now she remembered the secret thrill of pleasure that had run up her spine with self-disgust.

She had no right to reproach her parents for their clumsy attempts to kill the gunmen. For their abnegation of their humanitarian principles. Yet at the time her horror had been genuine and unsimulated. And ironically, it had earned her a place here at the heart of things. To live long enough to be one of their final hostages. To do . . . but what was there to do?

Rowena shook her head violently. As much at her own helpless thoughts as in reply to Shaw. 'No, of course, I didn't touch it. Why should I?'

'They're keeping the air lane free,' Richard said. 'That's why there's no traffic.'

Shaw nodded, drew in a deep breath, looked at his watch. 'The last few minutes are always the most difficult.' He took a pace forward and stood beside Richard. 'No more sign of your friend?'

'He's not *my* friend. But, no. He's gone.'

'Good!'

'How did *your* friend come to miss him?'

'He must have come through the woods.'

'Told you, didn't I? He'd be stopping up the earths. For the hunt. So the fox can't get to safety.'

Rowena watched her brother, wondering what, if anything, he was getting at. There were no hunts in July. Nothing til cubbing began in late October. Maybe he was just talking to steady his own nerves. He looked white as a sheet. Maybe he'd go to pieces in the end.

'Once they get a sight,' Richard spoke loudly, 'there's always a tremendous hullabaloo. The fox tries to take cover.' He looked over his shoulder at Rowena, in much the same imploring way she had looked at her father. He gestured downwards urgently with his hands.

She nodded. 'Cover,' she said. 'That's it! Take cover.

And that was all he was getting at. When the world is about to blow up around us, dear sister, take cover. Survive. We have been too stupid, too compliant to prevent this disaster, but lest any of the wreckage fall on our heads, take cover. Throw yourself down, wrench open the door, roll down the stairs. Escape.

'We must also cover,' Shaw said. 'Cover the last tracks.' He stood in the doorway, surveying Rowena's room. 'I want everything neat as a needle. If anyone comes here within the next three hours, tracks must be untraceable. The Greville family will have departed on its holiday. All will be normalcy.'

'The family will be in the cellar,' Rowena murmured softly, smoothing the coverlet on the bed in obedience to Shaw's pointing finger.

'And bloody uncomfortable,' her brother added.

Surprisingly, Shaw apparently conceded. 'You are right. Kuchi must go down and see that they are in no discomfort. Before we leave. As soon as our target is over the Outer Marker. Now please hurry! Time is of the primest importance.' He opened the door on to the landing and summoned Kuchi from his spy window.

The big red-haired man came in and put two spare valves and a coil of wire into a wooden case. He snapped it shut and straightened.

'That table,' Shaw hissed at Rowena. 'Tidy it more! You would not go away and leave jars thus unlidded!'

'I might.'

Shaw narrowed his eyes at her, but said nothing. He looked again at his watch.

'How long?' Richard asked.

'Our hour has come.' He crooked his finger at Hamid, indicated that he should leave the range-finder and come inside.

Just for a moment the three gunmen stood together in

Rowena's room. Solemnly they embraced. Even in this, their timing was perfect. The embrace was accompanied by the noise of amplified static.

Rowena caught her breath. She tried to stifle the hysterical scream that rose in her throat. Tried to avert her too revealing eyes from the balcony. Over the wooden balcony rail, a man's hand had appeared. Just visible beyond the three gunmens' shoulders, a dark, slowly rising head.

Simon.

Rowena closed her eyes, afraid to breathe. This time, even this too late time, she must not give anything away.

When she opened them again Shaw had spun round. For only a fraction of a second everyone stood quite still as he stood staring through the open french doors. 'Kill him,' he said to Kuchi, his voice rising to a crescendo. 'Kill him. Kill him. *Kill him!*'

And then she really did scream. So loudly that she almost drowned the laconic voice that came crackling out of the radio.

'Grantwick Approach . . . this is Speedbird Echo Foxtrot in the clear at Flight Level three eight zero. Heading one zero two. Estimate your field at zero three. Request descent clearance . . .'


'Out!'

It was the one word of English Kuchi appeared to know. Now he was in a hurry and he moved fast. He had opened the door, come down the cellar steps at double-quick time, loosened the cords round their legs six inches, roughly pulled them to their feet and pushed them forward.

Painfully and with difficulty, leaning against the wall, they managed to lift their feet up and mount the steps one by one. First Eleanor, then Mary, then Ginny, then Gordon several paces behind. Lastly, Kuchi yelling at them in a weird mixture of languages.

At the top of the stairs they assembled in a shuffling circle. None of his family said anything to Gordon. Mary turned her head towards him and wrinkled up her nose and gave him that funny little crooked smile that she always did when she knew he was low. He tried to convey something in his smile back at her, but then Kuchi was stamping around, shouting again and pointing, and in single file scraping their feet forward one behind the other, their hands still tied tightly in front, they moved out through the back door.

Gordon Greville lifted up his head and looked at the sky. About six hundred feet above the house was a blanket of cloud, pierced by tiny holes through which came slivers of sun. There was no sign of an aircraft. Five rooks quarrelled above the elm by the gate, and the rain still sparkled wet on the leaves of the beeches.

'Là . . . là!' Kuchi pushed Eleanor away from the rose-beds, pointing her to the left. Inch by inch, the little caravan, still in single file, edged round the corner of the house.

The Land-Rover had been taken out of the garage and was standing in the middle of the drive with its tailboard down and its engine running.

Still leading the way, clearly Eleanor thought that they were required to get into it. She had actually got hold of the side of the throbbing vehicle before Kuchi wrenched her hands off it, gesticulating and shouting 'Là . . . Là!'

Then he began pulling her over to the right, down the slope away from the garage and on to the turning circle.

There had been some more work done on it since last time, Gordon Greville noticed. Most of the turning circle had been completed. Under that part completed in the centre would be buried Mrs Bristowe and the babe. The ballast and tarmac had almost vanished. Only a cone-shaped pile of newly made concrete awaited them beside two wheelbarrows, three spades and a shovel. There remained to be done only a narrow slit trench, seven feet wide, eight feet long and three feet deep, wet and muddy.

They were halted on the edge. Kuchi was still at the leading end of the line, still holding on to Eleanor. He had begun gesturing towards the ditch.

Eleanor, not understanding, lifted her arms up at the back to show they were still bound and could not work. In reply, Kuchi pushed her roughly forward so that she fell into the trench. Then he got in himself and dragged her body hard against the end.

Moving a little away, he looked up. He held out his right hand and crooked the index finger at Mary, pointing to the space at his feet.

Obediently she jumped into the ditch. Obediently she lay down beside her eldest daughter.

Kuchi's eyes turned towards Ginny. He beckoned imperiously.

She stared back at him stonily, never moving.

He began to shout. He produced his Luger, waved it in front of her.

Just behind him, Gordon Greville waited. With great difficulty, he had dug the tiny cutting edge of the screwdriver into the rope on his hands, worked it to and fro until it frayed and snapped. Under the long sleeves of his old sports coat, his hands were free. At least he had been given an opportunity by Rowena – slender though the chances of success were – of saving them all. After the operation, the assassins would rely on two hours' confusion. A bomb on board would be the obvious suspect. By the time the authorities began to search the area, the cement would look dry and innocent enough. Their bodies would be buried beside Mrs Bristowe's. Enquiries would ascertain that the family were away on holiday.

Four would be dead. Two would be hostages. And the VC10 and all on board her would be destroyed.

Gordon Greville still waited. Kuchi's shouting had grown louder. The fat flesh on the back of the Albanian's neck had gone purple with fury. He took hold of the barrel of the Luger and raised his arm ...

Now, Gordon Greville said to himself, *now*!

Hatred gave him strength. Hatred made his mind clear, quickened his limbs. Not for a moment did the thought cross his mind that he could possibly fail.

His right arm shot out, grabbed the spade, turned it sideways. Then with both hands he raised it. For a fraction of a second, a shaft of moving sunlight glinted on the thin tapering steel.

Then the spade cleaved in the back of the Albanian's head.

Abruptly, the shouting stopped. The big man swayed. Bright red blood and grey brain came pumping through broken white fragments of bone. Then the legs gave way and he fell. The Luger clattered harmlessly down into the pit.

Immediately, Gordon Greville reached down for it, mindful of one thought now – to get up on to the balcony before the rocket could be fired.

But even as he scrambled in the mud and the rubble, he was conscious of the thunder of jet engines. Looking up, he caught a momentary glimpse of the tall red and blue top-hat tail of a British Airways VC10.

And seconds later he heard the explosions – one after the other – and he actually saw the thin silver rocket lift off above the house, and trailing its fiery tail, soar vertically up into the sky.


Rowena heard a sharp click, a *whooshing* noise. She stood frozen by the washbasin, a soaked sponge in her hand. As though in agonized slow motion, she actually saw the rocket leave the canister, trailing a wake of yellow flame.

So this was it. The worst had happened. The last-minute reprieve had not come. Of what use to have hoped at all? Of what use to speculate what Richard might be up to? Of what use to try to interpret his meaning of taking cover? Of what use to rejoice that Simon was alive? The gunmen would finish him off as soon as the Royal aircraft exploded.

Nevertheless, in the two seconds between first firing and the rocket motor igniting, she knelt down beside Simon and pressed the wet sponge to his forehead. He opened his eyes, gripped her arm and with an obvious effort drew himself up to a squatting position, screened by her bed from the view of the men on the balcony.

In the confusion of the last desperate minutes, they had flung his apparently lifeless body down there. It had all been done in silence.

'No blood,' Shaw had yelled at Kuchi. 'No blood!'

And no blood there had been. Just Simon, lying face down between her bed and the washbasin. Face downwards, big muscular arms flung out, limp and helpless. There had been a bruise on the side of his neck, that was all. In a little while, she had thought, there will be a dribble of blood from his nose or his mouth. There had been on Mrs Bristowe's body. I'm maturing fast. I am learning the facts of death, she had thought hysterically.

And having dumped him there, without another glance, Kuchi had opened the bedroom door, and gone thundering downstairs. Just before he closed the door shut behind him, she had seen him draw his gun. Or dare she hope to be truly mad? To have imagined it all? Her family weren't being massacred in the cellar. Her brother hadn't been suborned. Nothing like that could happen here. Not in England. Oh, there were odd bomb outrages, yes. But nothing like what happened in other countries. Even if the aeroplane had brought the world together, England was still a safe and sensible place. She was imagining things. She was mad.

She had bent down as the voice from the radio, Bill's measured sensible unhurried tones, announced, 'Speedbird Echo Foxtrot leaving the Outer Marker. Locked on Final.'

She had put her hand to Simon's bruised neck. It was warm. She had felt a pulse beat. He was alive. As in a dream, she had busied herself, not knowing really what to do. She had wet her sponge with cold water, and held it to his head. Again and again touched his lips with it. Then suddenly his eyes opened. She saw herself reflected in them. Dead eyes were milky, hazed, that she had also learned. Dark eyebrows now were raised in bewildered query. She whispered. Had she made him understand? He had only been half conscious and her story was garbled with fright. Drowned in the shout from Hamid at the range-finder. 'I see him! I have him!'

And then Shaw, still as a shadow, the rocket held against his shoulder. The metallic snap of the safety catch going off. Shaw's thumb on the radio direction control. Straightening up, she saw him press the trigger.

Now the second explosion, as the rocket motor fired. The noise dying away into the scream of four jet engines dead overhead.

Now, she thought, *now*. Now for the third explosion as the rocket connects and the aircraft blows up. She had a quick glimpse of Shaw frantically steering the direction finder. Then Simon must have grabbed her and thrown her to the floor. Here it came! A high whistling noise like a bomb falling! There was a bright oncoming light, as if the sun was expanding. She thought she heard Richard's feet running towards her.

The bright light exploded into a white magnesium flash. Smoke and the sound of falling masonry. The walls of her room seemed to be crumpling in. Hands were grabbing at her. She was choking, gasping for breath. All light vanished. She was in total darkness. Falling, falling, falling . . .

---

The radio voice was still talking. The bright light still shone Rowena could hear that brisk voice going cheerfully on. Other voices, not joining in, but speaking above it, urgently and yet quietly. Footsteps, movements. A door opening and closing. But all removed, the wrong end of telescope consciousness. The bright light was continuous. It neither wavered nor swelled. It came to her now, red as blood through her closed lids.

Some of that awful dusty smell still hung in the air. She shuddered, licked her lips. They didn't taste dry and dusty. Clean, sweet, tasting of the lavender soap her mother used, as if someone had washed her face. Tears swelled behind her closed lids. For many reasons, she didn't want to open them. She wasn't strong enough yet to see. Where was she? Was she in hospital? Was the bright light the lamp above the operating table? Was she the sole survivor of that awesome disaster? Had the aircraft crashed, the family been killed, and she, by some terrible unwanted fluke, been flung clear?

She tried to move her feet. They moved perfectly easily. Then her legs, her shoulders. She seemed to be all of a piece. She was lying on her side. Something soft pressed her left cheek. Moving air fanned the other. She heard the high warble of a robin. She thought she recognized her mother's voice. Then her father's. Or was it that voice on the radio? Music was coming out of it now. The National Anthem. A national day of sorrow beginning? No, cheering. Unmistakable cheering.

Very slowly, Rowena half opened her eyes. Big full-blown blue roses filled her vision. Blue roses hand-blocked on natural linen. The sitting-room sofa. She turned her head cautiously round. The french doors were open. A figure that could have been Eleanor was sitting outside.

No sign of wreckage. No sign of sun on mangled metal. She turned her head further round. Her parents were standing by the radio, talking in low voices to Richard. Everyone looked one distance removed, as if time had spun backwards and shrunk. She felt a quick lurch of relief, to be followed almost immediately by panic. Ginny? What had happened to her? What had happened to all of them? How did they come to be here? Where was the Royal aircraft?

As if she had shrieked the question aloud, the radio voice answered.

'And here comes Her Majesty now. I don't know if you heard the cheering? Despite the security precautions, large crowds have gathered. The Queen is descending the aircraft steps. A charming picture in the sunlight. Wearing what looks like cream wild silk . . . would you say that was what it was, Angela? . . . cream wild silk two-piece, with matching straw hat. She is smiling now, waving to the crowds. There, now you can hear the cheering!'

Rowena closed her eyes. Footsteps now. A shadow darkened her lids. She looked up. A face hung over her. Pale hair haloed in the full flood of sunlight behind.

'Ginny!' She went on repeating her sister's name, blubbing like an infant. 'It's just that I'm so glad you're here!'

'I never thought I'd see the day,' Ginny replied crisply, with something of her old elder-sisterly tone. Then the aptness of her own remark made her blue eyes cloud.

'Is Eleanor all right?'

Ginny nodded. 'Considering.'

At the sound of their voices, Mary Greville came over and sat on the end of the sofa. Gordon stood beside her, resting his hand on her shoulder. Richard remained by the radio trying to get louder reception. Out it came in a loud burst.

'. . . now Her Majesty is shaking hands with the crew. Captain Carter is presenting them each in turn to Her Majesty and she is no doubt thanking them all for a safe and happily uneventful flight. A smile for each of them. A few words with First Officer Waterhouse . . .'

For a moment Rowena thought, it has all been a dream. I have been the victim of an hallucination. Which is real and which is the dream? She reached out and held her mother's hand. 'What happened? Richard did something to the rocket, didn't he? But what? What *could* he do?'

'There is a device on most rockets,' Gordon said. 'A protection against shooting down friendly aircraft. It's called Identification of Friendly Forces . . . IFF. The aircraft transmits a signal that neutralizes the fuse. The terrorists were instructed to leave it alone. Fortunately it was a British rocket . . . one that Richard had seen at Farnborough. He tuned the frequency to what is called the squawk frequency that enlarges and identifies the aircraft signal on the radar. For full surveillance as always on Royal Flights, the squawk ident was transmitting and stopped detonation. The terrorists were told that this was used only in war. The identification of friend from foe.' Gordon looked down at his hands as he spoke to them, obviously deeply moved. 'But this *is* war, isn't it?'

Rowena nodded, acutely aware both of his distress and his dignity. 'And neutralized by Richard, then the rocket became a bomb. There was no wind, and it simply fell straight down again, exploding on impact. The balcony was blown up. Half the walls are down in your room. Shaw and Hamid killed.'

The band at Grantwick were striking up again. Over the radio boomed out the Stars and Stripes. The announcer's voice proclaimed: 'The Queen is shaking hands with the American

Ambassador. Both are smiling at the tribute of the music. The Queen has obviously made a joke. The Ambassador is laughing. The visit has certainly been an outstanding success . . .'

'And Simon?' Rowena asked looking at Ginny.

'He suspected something odd when I saw him in the village. Then from the woods he saw the glint of the rocket that Richard held up to use as a heliograph.'

'Is he all right? Where is he?'

'He's driven down to the village to get help.' A small smile touched Ginny's lips. 'He also managed to pull you and Richard clear, incidentally.'

'He must be as tough as old boots,' Rowena said, recovering and sitting up, feeling an almost hysterical euphoria taking over. 'He had a chop on the side of his neck that would fell an ox.'

'He's quite a man,' Ginny said.

'From you! Praise *indeed*!'

Ginny's reply was drowned in the announcer's voice.

'The Royal Daimler has now drawn up in front of the red-carpeted aisle from the aircraft. With a last wave, the Queen is stepping inside. The car is moving away between ranks of Coldstreamers. I can just see the wave of a hand. Tremendous cheering now! The band of the Welsh Guards.' The jolly beat of 'Colonel Bogey' echoed round the sitting-room of Fallowlands. No one spoke. The announcer's voice filled the room.

'Discreetly followed by two companies of the Gloucester Regiment. I don't know when I've seen so many police. Police lining the route. Police mingling in the crowds. This has been a great exercise in Security. After last month's incident at Heathrow, there has been no letting up. It has all been a great triumph for Security.'

'And for the family,' Rowena said. 'They were hell, of

course, but they had had their moments.'

'What about Simon?' Ginny said. 'He helped.'

'As I said, for the family,' Rowena repeated, smiling at her father. 'After all, it was the *least* he could do for his future in-laws.'